INN
SIGNIFICANT

A NOVEL

BY STEPHANIE VERNI

Book jacket designed by Stephanie Verni
Author photo by Matthew Verni

ISBN-13: 978-0692737439

ISBN-10: 069273743X

Mimosa Publishing

DEDICATIONS

To those who have loved, lost, and persevered.

To my students—do what you love and love what you do,
and remember, always continue to practice your craft.

To the people who live on the Eastern Shore of Maryland—
I love visiting your towns.

To the Sandaway Inn—thanks for the inspiration.

To my family...I love you dearly.
Thank you for supporting my passion for storytelling.

BOOKS BY STEPHANIE VERNI

Fiction

Beneath the Mimosa Tree

Baseball Girl

Inn Significant

Non-Fiction

Event Planning: Communicating Theory & Practice

(with Leeanne Bell McManus & Chip Rouse)

INN SIGNIFICANT

A NOVEL

BY STEPHANIE VERNI

SPECIAL THANKS

To my mother, Leni, and my husband, Anthony—
Thank you both for the special time
and care you took with this novel.

Prologue

The female officer gently taps Milly's face. The officer is talking to her, but Milly is struggling to decipher her words. Milly hears the commotion, and although the officer is only about a foot away, she sounds as if she is miles away. Her words are muffled.

"Are you with us, Mrs. Foster? Can you hear me?"

Milly moves her head slightly as the smelling salts stir her, and she indicates that she can hear, but she does not offer anything more than a slight raise of her right hand. She is incapable of movement beyond the exertion of what she has already done.

Milly is well aware that she is on the floor, spread across the hard, ceramic tile of her own foyer, the coldness of it pressing against her left cheek. She hears the shuffling of feet. Another voice is speaking to her. A male voice.

"Mrs. Foster, we're going to move you to the sofa," he says, his tone gentle. "We have some water for you."

Milly wants to remain just as she is and has no desire to relocate from the floor to the sofa. As she begins to come back from the blackness, her body feels limp and lifeless; she cannot move her limbs. If only she could be unconscious longer—if only she could pretend that none of what these people reported to her only moments ago is true.

The oven timer buzzes.

"It's in the kitchen," the female officer says. "Smells like something's in the oven."

"I've got it," the male voice says.

Milly hears the heels of shoes move along the hallway toward the kitchen. A drawer opens; an oven door slams. The smell of food wafts into the room, and she becomes queasy. She remembers putting a roast in the oven. That seems as if it happened days ago.

When she hears the feet from the kitchen shuffle back toward her, she feels the two officers grab hold of her under her arms and underneath her rear along her lower back in order to move her to the couch in the living room. Using one of the flatter, softer pillows, they prop up her head. Milly refuses to open her eyes. To do so would mean acknowledging reality, that which is true.

"We have reached her mother. She's on her way," says the male officer to the female officer.

Milly rolls onto her side. "I feel sick," she says.

"Paramedics are on the way," the woman says. "So is your mother."

"I don't want the paramedics. I don't want my mother. I want Gil!" she cries, as she brings her knees to her chest, curling into a ball and weeping uncontrollably. The echoes of her sobbing disturb the quiet of the house; they are eerie and heartbreaking.

The female officer crouches down next to Milly and holds

her hand. Tears form in the officer's eyes as she examines the bump on Milly's head. The officers could not catch her fast enough. She has witnessed inexorable pain on people's faces far too often in this line of work. After twelve years on the force, she wonders if it will ever become easier. Inevitably, she knows it's a rhetorical question, one she's asked herself far too many times.

"I know, Mrs. Foster, I know," the officer says, rubbing Milly's back. "I wish I could take the pain away for you."

Three weeks prior, Milly was in the hospital for a D&C; the baby she was carrying—the baby that would have belonged to Gil and her—had lost its heartbeat in her eleventh week. Milly thought the miscarriage was the end of the world; she couldn't have imagined it getting any worse.

But now she knows she is experiencing a most extraordinary nightmare.

Milly opens her eyes for a few seconds—long enough to glimpse the officer's face. For some reason, she wants to remember the kindness of the woman who, moments ago, on November 13, 2009, had the unenviable task of relaying the horrific and unimaginable news that her husband—her best friend, confidante, and most remarkable, loving man with whom she thought she would spend eternity—is dead.

CHAPTER I

The tragic reality about suffering the deaths of the baby you were carrying and your husband was that your heart broke into a million tiny, miniscule pieces, and yet it still wanted to be recognized as being alert...being present...doing its job. It, unfortunately, kept on ticking. Day after day you were forced to recognize the debilitating truth that the most important person in your life was dead, but you were not. Therein lay the great misfortune.

It was misfortune, indeed. First, because you were faced with a loss unlike any you have experienced in your life, and second, because you had the daunting task of having to carry on without him. Then, of course, what followed were the regrets and second-guessing of your past behaviors, your actions, your words, and everything you didn't do but should have said or done while he was alive. The amount of self-torture was unprecedented, and then as natural as the change of seasons, it became routine; it became a way of life.

This unfathomable situation is what happened to me. I started to drink more than I should have, and I didn't even care for alcohol that much. And I certainly wouldn't pass on the chance to take a long drag off a cigarette, either, even though I knew it had the potential to kill me. Maybe that's what I was hoping for. I cried a minimum of once a day. I was prone to catastrophic fits of anger, even going so far as to throw several plates against the wall, discus style, shattering them into pieces and shards. Immediately afterward, I did the most nonsensical thing. I laughed until I cried, sobbing for a solid hour on the cold, kitchen floor. Some might have called it utter madness. I recognized my despondent behavior, but I was unable to control it. And then, when the tantrum ceased, I allowed the pile of smashed debris to act as decorative litter for two full weeks.

Days later, my mother forced her way through the door.

"What the hell is going on here, Emilia?"

I could barely lift my head off the kitchen table. The kitchen was in complete disarray.

She picked up the ashtray at the end of the table and dumped it into the trash can along with the pack of cigarettes that was sitting beside it.

"And you don't smoke, remember?"

"I just don't care anymore," I said.

She tried to be gentle. Her worry for my state of mind was unparalleled; we were clearly in uncharted waters. Unfortunately, there wasn't a manual that offers suggestions to a mother on how to deal with her grieving child when the man her daughter loved more than life itself was dead.

For more than two years, I lived in a state of almost non-existence. Wearing pajamas all day and taking a shower once a week

had become bad habits. My friends all but abandoned me after trying everything they could to help me recover. I saw my friend, Angela, who doubles as my therapist, become frustrated with me in
sessions, even though I constantly and profusely apologized for the
repetitive nature of my dark thoughts and feelings. It was a daily
struggle to understand how one minute my husband was alive helping me get through a sadness we shared of losing a baby, and the next
minute, as I was preparing dinner, the doorbell rang, and I learned
that a tractor-trailer jackknifed, crushed my husband's car, and killed
him instantly.

I was unable to identify the exact moment that I finally
cracked and put the house up for sale. I just couldn't stand to live in it
any longer, even though it was practically paid off thanks to a fifteen-
year mortgage and a husband who made a lot of money working
as a government contractor. Once a dwelling full of happiness and
laughter, it became a morgue for me. I should have sold it sooner, but
I didn't know where to go or what to do with myself, quite frankly.
And then one morning, my mother called, which wasn't unusual at
all, because my mother always called. But on that particular day, she
had a motive for calling, and coincidentally, on that particular day a
couple of months ago, I happened to be curious and not depressed
enough to want to know what she had up her sleeve.

*

The plan my mother proposed to me required her to be incredibly persuasive, something that wasn't typically too challenging for my mother at all. She knew how to influence others when she needed to do so. I had to give her credit, though. She allowed me to work through my darkest times—always by my side, always with loving arms open or wrapped tightly around me when I wanted to shrivel up and die—and she understood I needed that time to be miserable. Of course, I knew she was worried. I was worried. I wasn't proving to anyone that I had the capacity to recover fully.

After months passed, although I began to come around slowly, my inability to become a fully functioning member of society was the last straw for my mother.

It was early morning, and I had just returned from seeing Angela; my eyes were bloodshot, a common occurrence that resulted from spending an hour each week lamenting about how joyful my life used to be when I lived with a man who effortlessly brought me love and happiness, when my mother called and begged me to meet her for lunch.

"You've got to eat, Milly," she said. "Please, just meet me for lunch. We can eat at that favorite place of yours—that little bistro place on the corner."

I love my mother. Her patience is astounding, and I had to remind myself that she was grieving, too. She lost a son-in-law, and one she liked quite a lot. When I was about to decline her offer, I remembered that fact.

"Ok. Food might not be a bad idea."

"So, that's a 'yes'? See you at noon."

*

A few hours later, I found myself standing at the hostess stand of the restaurant where I was greeted by a perky, curvy, twenty-something girl with tattoos running up her arm and on the side of her neck. She told me that my lunch date was already seated, and motioned for me to follow. I smirked as I watched the young hostess teeter in her spiked heels, as if she were wearing them for the very first time, like a little girl playing dress-up in her mother's heels. She looked a little ridiculous, and I wondered why on earth she would wear those spikey shoes to a job that required her to stand on her feet for most of the day. The hostess pulled out my chair at a table near the window with a view that looked across "M" Street and then walked away, her heels clicking on the uneven, hardwood floors.

"Hello, Mom," I said, planting a little kiss on her cheek before I sat.

"Hello, darling," my mother replied. "You're looking a little pale. You need to take yourself out of the house and enjoy some of the sunshine today; go for a walk and get yourself some Vitamin D. Good for the skin and good for the soul."

"Actually," I said, "it's not exactly good for your skin. You have heard of melanoma, haven't you?"

"Emilia, everything in moderation, and you'll be fine. You know that. Use a little sunscreen, maybe even a little foundation with some SPF, but get some sunshine. You could benefit from a little healthy glow in those cheeks."

I shot my mother a look through a crooked smile and picked up the menu. I began to peruse the choices, and zoned in on the shrimp Caesar salad and a cup of French onion soup.

"Look," my mother said cheerfully. "Before we even order— or actually, maybe we should have a glass of wine—I want to talk to you about something."

Once again, I was puzzled—first, by the lunch, namely because my mother had driven two hours that morning to see me. And secondly, because I was feeling a little anxious waiting for her to spill whatever it was she wanted to discuss with me. I was beginning to wonder what was going on in that peculiar brain of hers.

Before my mother could continue, the waitress took our lunch orders and my mother insisted that I have a glass of the house Pinot Grigio along with her. When the waitress walked away, I began fiddling with my silverware.

"Go ahead," I said. "Let's just get to it already."

"Okay, okay. I'm not going to beat around the bush. Here it is. Your father and I are going to spend some time out of the country, and I wanted you to hear it from me personally and not over the phone. It will only be for a year."

"What? Where?" I asked incredulously.

"Do you remember your father's friend, Devon? He's invited us to come and stay in their guest cottage in Ireland. He and his wife are opening a bed and breakfast and they want us to help out. We get to stay for free in return for the assistance."

"For a year?" I said.

"Yes. It's not that long."

"In Ireland?"

My mother looked at me from across the table, motioning for me to lower my voice, and giving the "shhhh" sign with her forefinger across her lips. Instantly, I was six again.

"Yes, sweetie, in Ireland. How's that for a new adventure for your mom and dad? So we're going to be gone for a while."

"What about the Inn?" I asked, unable to hide my astonishment and disbelief.

My mother uncrossed her legs and moved forward, leaning slightly on the table with her thin forearms. Her hair was pinned back in a loose bun, and her olive skin looked dewy and fresh in the light. She stared at me, took a deep breath, leaned back, and then folded her hands neatly on her lap in front of her.

"Well, that's just the thing. We want you to run it. We want to put you in charge of it. It's a little unexpected gift for you."

My jaw dropped open resembling a theme park clown's mouth at a squirt gun game, and for a moment, I couldn't believe this was her news. This was what she wanted to tell me.

"The Inn…a gift? Are you insane? I don't know how to run the Inn. I'm a writer."

"Ah…yes, you are. But at present, you're an unemployed writer who needs a big story. You stopped writing when—."

There was silence. She couldn't finish the sentence. Then, after the pause and our unspoken acknowledgment of what she didn't say, she continued. "I just need you to run the Inn during our absence. It may be a full year. You can do it. We want you to do it. We're asking you to do."

Whenever my mother became serious, I found myself wanting to panic. My mother, despite her unflappable ability to dream and her unique flair for the whimsical and all things positive, had been my rock and foundation my whole life—even when she drove me crazy—but in particular, I knew I couldn't have survived the past two years without her. I was having trouble wrapping my head around my parents' decision to tackle an adventure out of the country and leave me in control of their sole possession—the Inn that they single-handedly revamped into a successful business and life-style.

"Let's be serious and candid for a second, Emilia. You haven't been the same since it all happened. We know you've been through a lot. We've been through a lot. We know you're still suffering. You've had a couple of really dismal and challenging years. It's been awful. There's lots of stuff you still need to sort through. We get that. But guess what? Look at yourself. Under that sad exterior is the Milly who used to be. You're beautiful, fun, smart, and with a little sun-shine, your skin may glow again. You used to radiate happiness. I'm not saying you need to forget Gil—we never will. But it's been over two years and I just want to see you smile again. Like a real smile, remember? We want you to run the Inn. We've never asked you to do anything for us in our lives. But we want you to do this for us. I'm trusting you to do this for us."

The server interrupted her poignant oration by asking us both if we'd like anything else—bread, perhaps. We declined in uni-son, and she walked away, nearly falling over, tripping on the red car-pet that dressed up the hardwoods. In the past, a silly faux pas such as that would have had the power to make me giggle uncontrollably. Not any more.

I focused back on the question at hand, and I paused for a

second. For the last two years, I hadn't thought about anything but my own misery. I hadn't given anyone else's feelings any consideration. Truly. Sitting there at the table, across from my mother who was asking me for help made me realize just how absolutely self-absorbed I had been as I was caught up in my own sorrows.

My mother was asking me to do her and my father a favor. It wasn't that I didn't like the idea of the Inn. It was absolutely beautiful on a gorgeous piece of waterfront property on the Eastern Shore. My parents' way of life as proprietors of an Inn for the last ten years always fascinated me, and I was enormously proud of them for tackling the endeavor. Their lifestyle had always intrigued me on some level. My life in Washington, D.C. was so different from theirs. The business and bustle of D.C. was a far cry from the stillness and peacefulness found in a small town.

My mother had the amazing talent of playing the role of the consummate optimist—she always has. How was it that she could entrust her livelihood to a daughter who knew nothing about running such a place? How did she know I wouldn't run the damn thing into the ground?

She took a sip of her wine, and I realized she was patiently waiting for my reply. Maybe this was the answer, I thought. For months during my therapy sessions, Angela said that I needed to channel my energy into positive endeavors and stop living off the insurance money. I knew I couldn't turn down my mother's offer—her request. My mother was, indeed, correct about one thing: they've never asked me to do anything for them. Ever.

"How will I know what to do? I've only covered for you here and there," I finally said.

"It's easy," my mother said. "That's what John and Colette are for. They will walk you through it. They'll be with you every step of the way."

"Why? When do you leave?"

"In a month," she said. "Now that your house is sold, it is the perfect time for us to go before you buy another place for yourself. I know you've been looking for a property, but don't buy anything yet. Put your stuff in storage. Live at the Inn and figure things out."

I considered this impetuous decision and decided that my parents very well may have been certifiably insane. They were uprooting themselves for a bit, and with little notice.

"One month? That's a bit soon, don't you think? You assumed I would do this?"

"No," my mother said. "We were hopeful. We want to leave it in your care, not John's. You're my daughter. You deserve it. I know you'll be fine, and you can call me any time to ask me questions. John's been responsible for the check-ins, maintenance, and the daily tasks along with your father, and Colette will still run the kitchen.

She's organized. You'll see. Darlene works very part-time helping to clean the Inn. It really is more of a pleasure than a job. Why do you think we've been doing it for so long?"

I didn't want to take another bite. There was a deep churning taking place in the pit of my stomach, and I couldn't seem to breathe enough to get my heart rate to go down. I paused and looked at my mother.

"How can you leave me and move to Ireland?"

"Because it's temporary, Mill. We'll be back in a snap."

I wanted to believe her, but a sense of abandonment petrified me. I was a grown woman, and it made no difference that my mother could be abrupt, speak plainly, irk the hell out of me at times, and was the most annoyingly peppy person I knew, but she was my mother, and a girl always seemed to need her mother—and her father. But it was my mother who assumed the role of counselor during the entire tragedy.

Therefore, it was my mother who saw the concern on my face and became serious for a moment. "I would never abandon you. You and Gracie are my life…my blood. We just need your help for twelve months. This really isn't too much to ask, is it?"

"No, it's not. I'll do it, but I'm not sure you and Dad know what you're doing. Does Gracie know?"

"We called your sister last night and told her. She's only two and a half hours away, Mill, if you need anything. Just know she's there for you."

My mother paid the bill and we lingered for a few moments on the steps of the restaurant. "Let's set a few dates for you to come out and work with us before we go. You'll get the hang of it in no time. And, you'll stay in our cottage. I'll have all our things moved to storage, except for what we're taking, of course. You're going to be great at this. Think of all the stories you'll have to write. If you play your cards right, pay attention, listen with both of your ears, and actually use that beautiful leather journal I gave you last year for Christmas, you just may get an idea for an article—or a book—out of it," she said.

My mother winked at me. We hugged tightly, and I found myself practically clinging to her, a little lump building in my throat. When my mother began to pull away, I was tentative about letting her go. My head was spinning and everything was happening much too fast.

"Call me later and let me know which dates work for you to come to Oxford. We'll have you up and running in no time," she said.

I swallowed hard as I watched my mother walk to her car, her little figure moving farther and farther away from me. I smiled as I watched her get into her car. The breeze caught her hair and messed it up a bit as she eased into the driver's seat. The steadiness that is my mother could often be summed up in seven words: the unrelenting faith she had in me.

*

The movers were overly cheerful for movers. It made me wonder if they were aware of my situation. I tried my best to match their enthusiasm as they carried my possessions out and onto the medium-sized truck. I sold many of our belongings along with the house to the buyers. We purchased some of the pieces just to fit particular spaces, such as the round, maple dining table and six chairs, the white, custom-made armoire in our bedroom, and Gil's large desk. Would I have wanted to purchase the desk of the dead man who once lived in the house? I don't think I would have, because I'm superstitious when it comes to death and omens, but the new owners didn't have a problem with it at all. The rest of my possessions were being moved into one of those big storage units adjacent to the Capital Beltway.

I sat on the stairs and watched the movers carry out each item I had decided to keep. It made me second-guess everything. Why was I keeping any of it? Would there be a point in my life down the road when I would actually want to see the stuff again?

Being surrounded by items in the house day after day was just a constant reminder that there would be no baby and that Gil was gone. Purging myself of these physical belongings was perhaps something I was doing right, for once. Letting go of possessions meant letting go of reminders, and I hadn't done that since the accident. My mother was right. I'd held on to them for too long.

I followed the truck to the storage unit and it was filled up in no time. When they unloaded the last item from the truck and I closed and locked the door to the storage unit, I tipped the drivers and bid them well. In turn, they wished me the same.

Before I could leave the house for good, I had to stop back one last time to do a final clean and sweep. I settled on the property earlier in the morning, but the new owners were kind enough to allow me the rest of the day to get things in order. I would leave the other key on the kitchen counter; they had received the other two at closing.

As I pulled up to the house, it suddenly looked different to me. The front stoop looked naked without the potted plants, and I discarded the wreath that graced the front door. Several of my neighbors agreed to adopt the plants, as I didn't want to take them with me. The blinds on the windows were all up, having been thoroughly dusted, and the three-bedroom, white, Cape Cod-style house we owned in Washington, D.C. was now going to belong to a family of four.

I swept the house and cleaned every remaining nook and cranny for an hour. The bathrooms had been disinfected and scrubbed the night before, as had the kitchen, and I forced my broom into every corner, careful to have those floors looking as welcoming as possible. When I was finally done at six o'clock, I sat on the stairs and took one last look around. I prayed to Gil, asking him for forgiveness for selling this place—a home he loved so much and that had held so many fond memories for us, especially in the early years. There were some nicks on the floor where things had dropped, from gadgets to cans of food. The new owners would never know how each memory was made. The red wine stain on the hardwood floors was from a romantic evening we had spent together—the night I believe we conceived the baby. Then, I asked God why all of this had to happen. I hadn't received a reply or a sign yet, but I was left with no other option but to wait patiently for some insight.

The light streamed into the house, the evening sun pouring in through the curved bay window in the front living room. It was peaceful as it sat empty, waiting for its new owners to take hold of it, and I felt a moment of calm and serenity that I hadn't felt before when the house was full of belongings. And then the wave of guilt flooded me again, as it had so many other countless times before. I was leaving the only physical connection I had left to my husband, the person who always made me feel special and comfortable.

Farewell, my love.

I stood up, breathed deeply, wiped my tears, grabbed my broom and dustpan, and headed for the front door. As I cracked the door open, I looked around one last time and heard the voices that I sometimes heard when the world was quiet.

You're okay, Milly; you're okay, they said.

The door blew open, and then, I was gone.

CHAPTER 2

It was my fourth and final ride to the Inn in three weeks. I tossed the broom and dustpan into the back of the SUV, and started the journey to the Eastern Shore where I would make the Inn my semi-permanent home for the next year. It was a Tuesday evening in early May, and the GPS told me traffic was slightly heavy, and that I'd make it there in less than two hours.

I had said goodbye to my parents a few days ago, before the final move out of my house. They had asked me if I needed help, and I declined their offer. I'd been packing for the past two weeks, and there was little left to do. Besides, I wanted to let go of the house by myself. On the last trip I took to the Inn, I brought a few things with me and unloaded them there. During those three long days I spent with my parents, I received shotgun training on how to run a small hospitality business. I spent a little time with John, a man in his late thirties who was the assistant to my parents and who handled just about anything, and Colette, the feisty and bubbly 50-something cook who prepared the breakfasts and desserts and snacks for the Inn's guests. I'd known them both for years from my visits with my parents, and they are easygoing, nice people. John had been working there for almost three years; Colette had been around for five.

"I think you're going to be great at this, Milly-Bean," my father said to me after we'd gone over the books one last time. He ran his hand through his silver-grey hair and gave me a squeeze in the hallway. "You have a nice way with people."

"Thanks, Dad. That's a sweet thing to say considering I haven't even wanted to be around people for the last couple of years."

"We understand," he said, "more than you know."

He gave me a kiss on my forehead, and I thought the conversation would end there, but he guided me into the parlor sitting area, and motioned for me to sit on the loveseat. He sat down beside me and grabbed both of my hands.

"I just want to say this before we head off to Ireland. You've been struggling with so much, I never wanted to say this to you before, but besides your mom and your sister, you and Gil were the light of my life. He was like a son to me. There isn't a day that goes by that I don't think of him and miss him. It makes my heart hurt so much to think he is gone, so I can only imagine the depth of the pain that you have felt for the last few years. Honey, I love you. I want you to try to find some happiness here while we're gone."

My mother was always the one to say the right thing, to try to fix what was broken, or to help push me along, but these words, coming from my dad, were just so honest and kind, I could only lean forward and hug him. And then I cried. We both did, and it seemed to last for a very long time.

"What's all this going on in here?" I heard my mother say as she walked into the room and began plumping up pillows. The parlor had one, long, comfortable light blue sofa and several smaller, white reading chairs. There were built-in shelves on three of the four walls filled with books, nick-knacks, and photographs. She walked over to adjust one of the shelves, straightened out some books, and placed a couple of new magazines on the coffee table.

I was still hugging my Dad and gave her a "thumb's up," signaling all was well. She walked over to us both, stretched her arms around us, and kissed us each on the tops of our heads. "I don't even know what was said, but you're both making me teary. Don't let the guests see us this way. They may never come back," she teased.

We wiped our eyes, and my dad patted my head and wandered out of the room first. I hadn't quite expected to hear those sentiments from him, but it made me love him all the more. As for my mother, she did what she does best: she gave me a light tap on my bottom and said, "Chin up, Mills—this place needs you."

I grabbed a tissue and blotted my wet cheeks, trying to fix the mascara drips that ran down my face.

That was three days ago. My parents boarded the plane to Ireland late last night, and I received a text message earlier this morning that they had arrived. They were waiting to hear from me to let them know I had successfully made it to Oxford. As I drove the SUV out of Washington, D.C., I could feel the rattling of my bike against the trunk of the car. I wasn't sure if I'd secured it tightly enough—that was always Gil's job. He and I would take our bikes to the trails at Rock Creek Park or Great Falls Park and ride. Now, it was just my bike on the back of the car.

Now, it was just me.

*

Once I got out of the Washington, D.C. area and began the trek on Route 50, the ride to the Eastern Shore was pretty smooth. Passing Annapolis, I rode over the Severn River and could see the United States Naval Academy in the distance. A few miles later when I reached the Bay Bridge, early evening skies were clear and allowed for expansive views up and down the Chesapeake Bay. Sailboats and powerboats glided along the Bay, and the sun was setting behind me. Once on the bridge, I knew there was less than an hour remaining, but I didn't mind at all. I was listening to John Mayer and enjoying driving with the windows down, feeling the breeze in my hair, and executing the breathing exercises Angela taught me. I wasn't particularly stressed at that moment, but I found the technique helpful in all situations, especially ones in which you realize you are about to embark on a wholly new experience and lifestyle.

Breathe, I told myself. *Just breathe.*

As the Bay Bridge meets the land on the Eastern Shore, it's as if you landed in a different world. Immediately, I felt the slower pace of life. Living in the D.C. area was hectic; there was unbearable traffic, a rushed pace of life, crowded stores and restaurants, and a constant hum of roadways. There was light traffic on Route 50, but most of those travelers were heading to the Maryland and Delaware beaches—Ocean City or Rehoboth or Bethany. I took the exit to-ward the town of Oxford. The Inn was located on the water just a stone's throw away from the ferry at the Port of Oxford. It was when I turned right on S. Morris Street that my adrenaline began to pump.

When I saw water in front of me, I made the left on West Strand Street, and approached the Inn. There was a new sign hang-ing off the tall picket fence that bordered the property. I could barely make it out, but once I got closer, the light went on just above it and I could read it clearly. "WELCOME," it said in bold print. And then underneath that word, in a pretty script font, was the name of the Inn: INN SIGNIFICANT.

The driveway curved a bit, and I pulled along the gravel road up near the Inn. Multi-colored, helium balloons were tied to the railings on the large front porch—at least ten of them—with a big banner across the porch that read, "Welcome, Milly!" I couldn't be-lieve my eyes. I put the car in park and just sat and looked at it. With trepidation, I exited the car and did something I hadn't done in two and a half years: I grabbed my iPhone and took a photograph of those balloons and that sign. I don't know what prompted me to do so, except that for some reason I wanted to remember that particular moment. I stood and stared at it, leaning against the SUV. I was afraid to walk through the door and begin the new "adventure," as my mother kept calling it. But there was something magical about that particular scenario that just felt like going home, even though I had never actually lived in the place. I had, however, visited quite a lot over the years, and there was a great deal of family history tied to it.

The door flew open and John appeared, bounding swiftly down the stairs.

"You made it!" he said with a smile on his face, his hand raised with a wave. "Welcome!"

"Thanks, and thanks for that," I said, pointing to the balloons and sign.

"I wish I could take credit for it," he said, "but your mom and dad and Colette masterminded it. But I figured I'd come out and admire it with you. All I did was hang the banner."

"A-ha," I said. "So you see, you did have something to do with it. It was a sweet gesture."

"It was. And now I'm here to offer another one. How about some help getting all those bags to your cottage?"

"I would love it," I said.

*

My mother and father had two small cottages built on the property that were adjacent to the Inn. One was theirs; the other was John's. Colette did not live on the property, but resided in a house a few blocks away in town with her husband. Her children were grown; one lived in the area, and one settled in Florida with her husband. My parents' cottage had four rooms—a living room, a kitchen and eating area, and a master bedroom and bath. John's cottage was a mirror image of it. My parents wanted to live on the grounds, but not live in the house that was the Inn. That original structure belonged to my grandmother and grandfather, who both passed away twelve years ago, one right after the other. They owned the property since they were young, all seven acres with three acres of waterfront on the Tred Avon River. It was a spectacular piece of land. When my parents inherited the property, they discussed what they wanted to do with it. They considered selling it, and knew its incredible value. Something kept telling my mother that putting it on the market wasn't the right thing to do. When it dawned on them to give hospitality a try, my mother began her research. My father talked to people, applied for their business license, hired contractors, and little by little the idea of giving the Inn a whirl appealed to them both. Within months, my parents sold their house in Annapolis, and put the money they reaped from the sale of their own home, along with the money they inherited, into the construction of the two little cottages and the renovation of the existing home that my grandparents lived in for of all their lives. My father kept his job as a boat salesman for several years to keep the cash flowing, but my mother stopped teaching to give the Inn her full attention. He also received a sizeable inheritance from his own parents, who owned several small businesses in Pennsylvania. After thinking it through carefully, they were convinced that creating an inn of significance that was incredibly welcoming in Oxford would be a great way to spend their days while also enjoying the splendor of living on the water in a town they loved.

John helped me unload my things and we set them all in the living room of the cottage. The pile of stuff was growing, even though I had purged many of my things and brought very little with me. French doors in the living room opened to a small patio, replete with two lounge chairs, a bistro set, and large potted plants around the edges. It was quaint, and a small, white picket fence surrounded the charming patio area for a little privacy. I saw all the potted plants and hoped I wouldn't do them any harm; it was time to find my green thumb again.

"What's that?" I said, pointing outside.

"Why don't you go take a look?" he said. He flicked on the patio light, and there was an adorable, pink beach bike, with a wicker basket on the front of it and a wire basket mounted to the rear. My name was painted on the bar, and it was wrapped up in a big, yellow bow.

"I brought my bike," I said. "Is this from my parents?"

"Yes," he said. "But yours seems to be more of a mountain bike. This one is meant for town. You can't live here and not have a basket on your bike, Milly."

"Well, look at that," I said, walking around it, checking it out. "Two surprises in ten minutes. It sure is cute. Do you have a basket on your bike?"

"Um, no. I'm a guy. I ride with a backpack. What would the townspeople and guests say if they saw me on a cute, pink bike with a basket?" He was teasing, and it actually made me laugh.

"I see," I said. "We won't question your masculinity."

"Please don't," he said. "Haven't you noticed my muscles bulging as I've carried in each of your items?"

He was poking fun at himself, because he didn't look like a weightlifter, but he had a slender build and looked strong. His hair was brown and cut short, and he had a rich tan despite that it was only May in Maryland.

"Well, I thank your muscles for moving me in tonight."

"My pleasure. So, just a couple of quick things. Your phone has a direct line to my room—you just need to hit #2. You are #1. The office and front desk is #3. We have to interview those two college students in the morning who want to work the desk for the summer. One is coming in at 10 a.m. and the other is at 11 a.m. Your fridge has been stocked with some basics. Colette got you milk, eggs, bread, fruits, cereals, and some yogurts to get you started tomorrow morning, then we can do a big list and get your food. You can also eat breakfast at the Inn if you want. Don't feel like you have to stay in your room. And let me know if you need helping hanging anything in your room once you get adjusted."

I looked at him for a second, taking it all in, and feeling a little pampered.

"Remember, I work here, so you don't have to treat me like a guest," I said, "but I sure do appreciate all the attention you and Colette put into all this."

"It was our pleasure. Do you need help putting anything away?"

"No," I said, looking around the room at the piles of stuff I brought. "I'll take my time getting things in order. Thank you so much, John."

He started to walk toward the door. "Just let me know if you need anything else. See you in the morning."

"Will do," I said. "See you in the morning."

When the door closed behind him, I heard his footsteps as he walked away. I also heard the silence that was only brought to life by crickets, cicadas, frogs, and the slushing sound of the river. It was the sound of nighttime on the Eastern Shore.

I wondered how I would sleep listening to the quietness of nature's symphony.

CHAPTER 3

When the sun rose in the morning, so did I. I slept well, but being in a new environment—in my parents' cottage—had me up earlier than expected. It was cozy, and I had put away a lot of my belongings before I went to bed. I had stayed up late getting things in order, placing clothing in drawers and in the closet, organizing some of the kitchen items I brought with me, and displaying the pictures in frames I deemed not too depressing. As I stepped out of bed, I decided not to shower just yet, but instead climbed into some sweatpants, flip-flops, and put my hair in a ponytail. I grabbed my sunglasses, and walked outside to sit along the water for a few minutes before I started the day.

As I wandered outside, I realized I wasn't alone. An older couple, obviously guests at the Inn, were sitting in the Adirondack chairs sipping their coffee. I smiled when I saw them there. The scenery was incredibly inviting. The Inn and its tranquil location had the power to lure people to spend time on its small, sandy beach, relax in the chairs that graced the meticulously manicured lawn, read in the hammock set between the trees, ride bikes, or take leisurely strolls into the small town for a bite to eat. I had heard the stories from my mother over the years: visitors come and go, and more often than not, those visitors came back.

I wondered if it were that couples' first time at the Inn. It made me envious that I would never have those types of moments with Gil. I'd always imagined growing old with him. He loved to travel, and the trips we took were some of the best times of our lives. We sipped Champagne in outdoor cafes in Paris; we biked the hills of the Cotswolds in England; we ate our own picnic lunch along the Arno River adjacent to the Ponte Vecchio in Florence; and we lounged with Pina Coladas in our hands in St. John's. I experienced great love and romance on those trips, and desperately questioned how it could all vanish in a flash. I wondered if the couple had children and how old they might be; if only I hadn't suffered a miscarriage, I'd still have a piece of Gil with me, a child that we had made together. The woman held her cup of coffee near her chest, and threw her head back in laughter. The husband patted her knee and they smiled at each other. How lucky they were—did they know just how fortunate they were to have each other?

The water was calm, as it tended to be in the early morning as the dew clung to the grass and the birds sang their morning songs. I kicked off my flip-flops and walked on the sand of the short beach and stuck my toes in the water. It wasn't as cold as I'd imagined it would be. Maryland had experienced an unusually warm May thus far, and it must have helped the temperature of the river. I stood with my back to the Inn, facing the expanse of the river, and I practiced the breathing exercises my therapist taught me. For me, it was a form of meditation. Breathe in, breathe out. Inhale deeply, blow it out.

The rising sun warmed my face, and it felt good.

*

At eight o'clock, I walked through the front door of the Inn. I was showered and dressed for the day. I pulled my hair up into a bun because the thought of blow drying it and fussing with it was too much. I wore a red pencil skirt with a white blouse and pointed flats. I even put on a little bit of makeup. My mother had been right, of course: I could use a little sunshine on my face.

The smell of bacon lured me past the parlor and through to the kitchen prep area.

"Good morning!" a voice called from behind the stove. Colette was flipping some pancakes, a big bowl dripping with batter next to her.

"Good morning," I said. "And thank you for the lovely welcome on the door last night. It was very sweet of you and my parents."

"No problem," she said. "We're excited to have you. Have your parents made it to Ireland?"

"Yes," I said. "I just hung up with them a few minutes ago. They made it fine. They said the weather is good right now."

"That's wonderful." Colette placed the cooked pancakes in a white serving dish. "I've got another twelve done. Would you mind taking these into the dining area, Milly, and putting them in the warming pan?"

"I'd be happy to," I said.

I walked into the dining room where two couples were enjoying their breakfast. Colette set out quite a spread. There were handmade scones and muffins, fresh fruit in cups, bacon, scrambled eggs, and these extremely dense buttermilk pancakes. On the adjacent table sat small boxes of cereals with fresh milk, and coffee and tea, with today's brew of hazelnut filling the room with its scent. Colette placed fresh flowers in vases on the tables.

I said hello to the couples and chatted with them for a few minutes. One couple was from Virginia, the other from Delaware. Both were planning to take the Inn's bikes for a ride and then board the ferry to St. Michaels. It certainly was a good day for it. The sun was shining, it was eighty-two degrees, and there was no humidity in the air.

Back in the kitchen, I asked Colette if there were anything I could help her with as she cooked up a storm. She told me to sit with her, have a fruit cup and a muffin.

"Thanks, Colette," I said. "A little fruit would be nice."

"I can't take credit for the muffins," Colette said. "Those are all John."

"John bakes?" I asked, raising one eyebrow.

"They're his specialty. He sneaks in here in the evenings sometimes and makes a bunch. The guests love them. Some secret family recipe."

The oven timer went off. Colette bent down to see if it was ready.

"Looks like it's done," she said.

"What is it?"

She pulled out two sumptuous looking loaves of bread, their tops perfectly browned. "One's cinnamon and one's cinnamon raisin," she said.

Colette began to ease them out of the pans with her long knife. They were placed on two beautiful wooden bread blocks. She glazed them both, and I couldn't resist giving the baked bread a try after she sliced them.

"This is fantastic," I said. "Gil would have loved this."

When the words flowed out of my mouth, I knew I shouldn't have said it. I didn't want to make Colette uncomfortable, and I had sworn that I would keep my grief to myself and not allow anyone else to feel sad for me. How was it that within seconds of sitting with her, I blurted something out about Gil? I immediately regretted it. I was the one grieving still, but I didn't need to bring everyone else

around me down. Angela mentioned this to me a thousand times—
people deal with grief differently, and you can't force others to grieve
the same way you do. We all cope in different ways. Lately, I'd felt
the need to talk about Gil. Somehow, it made me feel better. My sister, Gracie, would lend an ear whenever she could, in between caring
for her adorable one-year-old daughter.

Colette paused, stopped what she was doing, and looked at
me, not with pity or sadness, but with a glint of understanding. "He
was a wonderful man," she said. "I bet you miss him terribly."

"He was the best husband," I said, tears starting to build. "I'm
sorry I mentioned it."

"Are you kidding? Don't ever be sorry for missing someone
you love and wanting to talk about it. I remember when you both
would come and visit. I can picture Gil and your dad crabbing on the
dock. He did love this place. They never caught much, but the two of
them had fun together. I'm so sorry for your loss, Milly. I hope being
here with John and me gives you a little bit of comfort. We love your
parents so much; they have mourned, too, and they hate seeing you
suffer. Anything we can do for you, you just let us know. Okay?"

She patted my arm and looked me straight in the eyes. I
couldn't help myself. I leaned in and gave Colette a big hug. I wasn't
trying to be morose; sometimes I just want to remember that Gil
was here…that he loved, ate, drank, laughed, was silly, and said the

stupidest things sometimes, but he was my happy, silly person. The depth of my love for him was tough to put into words.

However, I could admit one thing: eating that cinnamon raisin bread with a cup of tea while talking to Colette made all the hurt I still kept inside feel just a little bit less.

*

After I helped clear the dishes in the dining room and straightened up the eating area when the guests were done, I checked the guest reservation book. The couple I saw earlier on the lawn drinking coffee checked out, and we had two new guests arriving today. The Inn had six rooms, which were renovated by my parents when they took over the place. Each room was decorated differently, and each had its own private bath. My mother loves cottage style, so the rooms were either painted white or a light blue, the furniture was white or a light pine, and chandeliers were centered on the ceiling in each room. The distressed furniture added to the comfortable style, and she had bought floral linens and white comforters for the beds. She'd added a splash of color with pillows, and draped the windows with pink, purple, light green, or light blue sheer curtains. One last touch she included were fresh flowers in each room on the bureau and a welcome basket with a bottle of wine. "Adding the baskets and the fresh flowers are the Inn's personal touch we provide each guest," she told me as she gave me my instructions.

On the other side of the house, my parents added on a room that serves as the laundry and storage room. The dimensions are equivalent to that of a good-sized family room. When the guests checked out, it was my job to strip the sheets, throw them in the wash, remake the beds, dust, vacuum, tidy the room, and get it prepped and ready for the next check-in. The regular housekeeper, Darlene, was away for three weeks on a vacation visiting family in Canada. Because there were only six guest rooms and people arrived and departed on different dates, for the next few days, it wouldn't be too taxing. However, one of the two jobs John and I were interviewing for was additional housekeeping help. We agreed that an additional person to help with housekeeping would be a bonus, although it certainly wasn't necessary.

I was coming down the stairs with a laundry basket of sheets when I saw John come through the front door.

"Good morning," he said. "Did you sleep well?"

"Not too bad for my first night," I said.

"I got the Dawson's bags into their car. They are on their way to your old stomping grounds—Washington, D.C.—for a couple of days."

"That's nice," I said.

"Here, give me that basket," John said as I hit the second to last step. "I'll take it to the laundry room, and then I'll meet you in the office for the interviews?"

"Sounds good," I said.

*

The office was located in an adjacent, smaller building. There were two desks inside; one was a taller, white countertop desk with beadboard on the front and a high stool; the other, set across the room, was an antique pine desk. Again, the office was light and airy, and my mother had built-in bookshelves along two walls with batten board from floor to ceiling on the other two. The wrought iron chandelier that illuminated the pine desk was purchased at an antiques store in St. Michaels. I was with her when she bought it. The other chandelier was custom-made by a design student the summer before Gil died. The college girl was studying art design in Baltimore and needed a project for the summer. My mother, always one to help out a friend or neighbor, was the guinea pig. Or so we thought. Once the student got her grade for her project—no doubt an "A"—the chandelier found its home in the office. My mother has remarked on several occasions that it's one of her favorite pieces she put into the décor.

Karen entered the office and sat between John and me. She was a petite, blonde girl with a big smile. Her family lived nearby and she was home for the summer from college. My parents knew her parents, and she had inquired a couple of times about working at the Inn. Both John and I liked her a lot, and she applied to be the Inn's receptionist and part-time office manager.

"We'd also like you to work one night a weekend and one night during the week, so that Milly and I can actually have a bit of time away from here. That means that you would be in charge while we are out. Does that work for you?"

Karen was happy to oblige, and it made me realize that running an Inn does require you to be on call twenty-four hours a day. I never even considered having "free time," primarily because I had no social life to speak of, but John clearly did. He wanted to be able to do things a couple of nights a week, and even get a day or afternoon off once a week. I couldn't blame him; no one should have to work all the time.

"We always have our cell phones on us if you need us," he further explained to Karen. "So, if something comes up, don't hesitate to call."

We thanked Karen for coming and said goodbye to her; we told her we would call her as soon as we made a decision. There was little to discuss because she was bright, amenable, and appeared to be conscientious, with a resume that backed it up. I volunteered to call her two references.

Then, we waited for the second candidate to arrive. By eleven forty-five, John and I realized candidate number two was not going to show at all, and I quickly began to seek input from Karen's references. Within an hour, references were checked, Karen was called, and we had a summer employee lined up. So far, it wasn't a bad morning at all.

I spent the afternoon helping Colette make the next grocery list, straightened up the parlor and changed the linens on the tables. The skies outside were bright blue, and the sun twinkled on the water. At that point, I decided to make sure the furniture on the back patio was clean and that the cushions were on the chairs.

John was tending to the gardens, adding colorful plants to the flower boxes outside. I breathed in the scenery. Why hadn't I spent more time here? I'd visit now and then since my parents owned the Inn, but I hadn't appreciated it as much as I did at this very moment. Tranquil and simple. There was something entirely refreshing about it. It made me think of the house I left behind and whether or not the new owners would be happy in it. I certainly hoped so.

"Do you approve?" John called to me, bringing me back from my straying thoughts, pointing to some of the flowers he was potting.

"You have a good eye," I said, walking closer to him. "I can help with the upkeep of these. I'm actually not too bad at not killing plants."

"That would be great. I'm good at planting, and continuously work on improving my skills at keeping things alive. Feel free to alter anything at any time," he said. "We got all these flowers last weekend from the fundraiser flower show in Easton, and I've been meaning to get to it, but it was a little hectic when your parents were packing up to leave."

"I can imagine. Are all their things in storage on the grounds?"

"Yes, it's all here; some of it is in the shed, and the rest is in cartons and boxes in the laundry room and basement. Have you taken your bike for a spin yet?"

"No," I said. "Not yet. Just getting acclimated here. I'm excited about Karen. She seems like a nice girl."

"I agree. Good pick. She starts Monday?"

"Yes. Monday at 8 a.m."

"Well done, Milly," he said.

I felt a strange sense of accomplishment. I hadn't done all that much today, but I did a few things: I helped with breakfast and clean up, made the list of groceries we needed for the next few days, cleaned and tidied a guest room, as well as the parlor and dining room, interviewed a candidate for the front desk, and spent a few moments seeing what was coming up for the rest of the week. I couldn't remember the last time I felt useful and productive.

John stood up and walked over towards me. "I don't mean to ask a million questions, but I was wondering…I wanted to ask you…" He seemed hesitant to say what was on his mind.

"Go ahead. Feel free to ask me anything."

"I like to get a little exercise in each day and didn't know if you did, too. Since we both can't be gone at the same time until Karen starts her job, do you mind if we set a schedule so one of us is always here, especially when Karen is not working?"

"Of course," I said. "I'm not a die-hard exerciser, but I probably should be. Tell me what time you typically like to exercise, and I'll be sure not to schedule anything so I can cover the desk."

"Guests typically don't arrive very early in the morning because our check-in is at noon, so how would you feel about me getting it in between six-thirty and eight? That gives me time to exercise and shower."

"I feel fine about that. I never have been, and never will be, an early-morning exerciser. Afternoons work best for me."

"Sounds like a match made in Heaven," he said.

CHAPTER 4

Lunch and dinner are not served at the Inn, but at four in the afternoon each day, the Inn offers afternoon tea. Colette stayed late on my first day to show me how it's done, although she prepares everything but the hot water ahead of time. I set everything on the tables in the dining room, and guests are free to take their drinks and food to the porch. Afternoon tea consists of scones, cucumber and salmon bite-sized sandwiches, homemade cookies, and the cake or pie of the day, as baked by Colette and decided by her own whim. For years, she worked at a bakery, and that was her original passion, although she confessed to me as we set up the tables that working at the Inn was her favorite job she's ever held.

"I like getting going in the mornings and being done by early afternoon. Your parents are so sweet to set up the afternoon tea—all I have to do is have everything ready for them, and they take care of brewing the tea. It's lovely to work with them, and I enjoy the guests who come here. By and large, they are all terrific people. I mean, you get your odd duck every once in a while, but that's what makes the world turn, right Milly?"

"I suppose so," I said with a chuckle.

"How are you liking your cottage?"

"Well, so far, so good. I need to get a little more settled. I put a lot away last night, but I have a few more things to sort later on."

I straightened out the tablecloths and set out the plates, tea-cups and drinking glasses, napkins and silverware on the antique server my mother won at a local auction. The dining room was charming. It was light and airy, with white, detailed wide-plank batten board. There was a built-in white cabinet with crystal pulls where the food was set. In the glass doors of the cabinet were the China, teacups, and glasses, and the silverware was stored below in the drawers. The ceiling was made of rich pine with tin tiles for detailing. My mother and her interior designer created a great space, modeling it after a photograph my mother had ripped out of a magazine. Two bright, large chandeliers hung in the room. I always teased my mother about her obsession with chandeliers—she wanted one in every room, and I had to give my dad credit, because he let her decorate the place the way she wanted. In the end, he was incredibly pleased with how the Inn turned out, and instead of calling the Inn a cottage, he seemed to prefer to call it "the castle that Mom built."

Three of the four couples staying at the Inn showed up for the afternoon tea. I could tell Colette was tickled pink by all the compliments regarding the food, and she even made a big pitcher of lemonade in case there were no takers for hot tea on a warm day.

By five o'clock, she left to go home, and as I was putting things back in the refrigerator, I noticed she left something there for John and me with our names on it. "Enjoy your dinner," she wrote on the note. It turned out, she had made a big dish of lasagna and split it down the middle for each of us to take back to our cottages.

*

In the evening, after I'd tidied up the office and forwarded the Inn's line to my cottage number, I slipped into my comfortable loungewear and curled up with a book. I had just finished two chapters when there was a knock at the door. It was nine-thirty at night.

"Milly? It's John," he said through the door.

I opened it, and he was standing on the small porch in comfy shorts and a snug "Just Do It" t-shirt in his flip-flops.

"Hello," I said, slightly embarrassed. I wasn't expecting to see anyone at that hour, and I was not wearing a bra under my shirt. I crossed my arms to hide my chest.

"Colette told me you were a little surprised that I am ultra-talented and know how to make muffins. I was wondering if you wanted to join me as proof that I am, in fact, the midnight muffin-maker."

The gesture made me a little uneasy, and I immediately felt guilty as I caught a glimpse of the photograph I placed on the small bookshelf of Gil and me at a neighborhood barbecue staring me in the face.

"Um, I—"

"We're just going to make some muffins and chat. That's all," he said, apparently cognizant of my reluctance and respectful of my past life. Shortly after Gil died, I had visited the Inn and stayed with my family. John had offered me his heartfelt condolences, and we never spoke of it again after that. As a young widow, I found that people just don't know what to say sometimes, and not addressing it was just so much easier. I completely understood that.

"Okay, but I'm dressed like this. Do I need to change?"

"Nope. Come as you are, that's what I always say. It's important to be comfortable because in this business, late night is the only time of the day when you really get your own time. Plus, don't you remember being a kid and sneaking down into the kitchen after your parents had gone to bed for a little midnight snack? We're kind of doing that as grown-ups."

I giggled. I remembered doing that a couple of times in our home in Annapolis when I wanted to watch something on television, but my parents wouldn't let me stay up late. After they went to up to their room, I would tip-toe down the stairs, grab cookies and milk, and sneak to the basement where I turned the television on very softly. Invariably, my mother was smarter than I thought she was. "Did you enjoy watching *Saturday Night Live* last night?" she would ask the next morning.

"Yes, I did that a few times, but I always got caught," I said. "I'm not much of a schemer, I'm afraid."

"No chance of getting caught tonight, seeing as how your parents are in Ireland."

I looked at him for a moment, grinning. At that instant, I felt a spark of childish madness come over me. I couldn't believe I was living here and doing this. It was absolutely insane.

"Okay, let me just get myself together, and I'll meet you up there," I said.

*

The night air was surprisingly cool, and there was a soft breeze blowing as I walked up to the Inn. It was picturesque at night; the skies were clear and the stars were out, twinkling over the water. The Inn itself glowed with soft lights on the front porch and some lighting along the gardens. I was wearing my Old Navy lounging bottoms with a worn-out *Wicked* baby doll tee, but made sure to put my bra back on underneath it. I'd seen *Wicked* in the theatre five times, my all-time favorite Broadway show. Gil even went with me one time.

The kitchen area was humming, and the radio was playing. The first thing I noticed when I walked in made me chuckle: John was standing at the counter wearing an apron.

"Domesticated, I see," I said. He smirked.

A man in command in the kitchen was not something I was used to at all. My neighbor's husband was a chef and made all the meals for the family. I always remarked to her how wonderful that must be. Gil never had that particular talent or interest, though he had many others that made up for it. I made the breakfasts, lunches, and dinners. There was Italian blood in me from my mother's side of the family, and I learned how to cook from her. My father had never been domesticated until he owned the Inn. Then, he started to become more familiar with the kitchen. And he cleaned. And did laundry. Sometimes people do change.

I watched John move around with ease, almost ambidextrous in nature, gliding around effortlessly, pulling items and food from cabinets and pantries. He opened the oven to check the temperature. He mixed up a gooey batter in a sturdy, red mixing bowl with a matching red Williams-Sonoma spatula.

"I'm sorry. I already started the process when I decided to knock on your door," he said. "This batch is mixed."

He filled the muffin cups with the batter, letting it pour into each cup, and when they were all filled, he slid the entire tin of what looked like perfection into the oven.

"Would you care for a cup of tea?" he asked, attempting to conjure up a British accent. It didn't go too well, and we both smiled.

"Yes. Decaf, please," I said, attempting to produce a similar accent in response, but failing miserably at it.

"Got it," he said as he began making it.

"I feel silly just sitting here not helping."

"Don't. It's my grandma's recipe, and because a little birdie told me you didn't try one this morning, I'm going to make you try one as it comes out of the oven. Your mother told me that your writing career began with food reviews. I'm looking forward to your verdict."

"That was a long time ago, when I actually was a writer and it meant something."

"I understand," he said. "But I'd still like to hear your review of Grandma's muffins."

"I'm feeling extraordinary pressure to like them," I said.

"The word 'like' shouldn't be a part of your vocabulary when you're describing treats you will salivate over," he said with a wink. "That's something you do on Facebook. As a writer and former food critic, I expect a far more elaborate and eloquent dissection and analysis of the food from you."

"I'm better on paper," I teased.

When the timer went off, he pulled the first batch out of the oven, steam rising off the tops ever so slightly, and then sat across from me at the table.

"Have one of these," he said, and he placed a hearty, substantial treat onto my delicate plate adorned with roses.

"A crunchy muffin?" I asked. It appeared to be hard on the bottom with some sort of loose, sugary topping that resembled a crumb bun on top.

"Grandma will want to know if you like her recipe."

"Is your grandmother still with us?"

"Yes, she's alive and pretty well at the young age of eighty-four. She lives in the assisted living place, Heartfields, down the road. I'm sure you'll meet her at some point."

As I peeled the paper away from one half of the muffin, and then leaned in to bite into it, my taste buds tingled at its sweetness, but it was dense, too. It unexpectedly melted in my mouth. I unpeeled the paper away from it entirely and took another bite. John watched me with anticipation, his eyes wide, as I fluttered my eyelids in a euphoric state, licked my lips, and began to formulate an opinion. He motioned for me to comment regarding its taste with his raised eyebrows, even though my mouth was full of food. I was having fun toying with him a little bit as I kept him in suspense.

"Well, it's certainly crunchy. I like the crumbly mix on top... it tastes like pleasure and trouble all rolled into one."

"Pleasure and trouble?" he asked.

"Yes, pleasure, because it tastes heavenly, and trouble, because tomorrow my thighs will curse me."

I sipped my tea as I enjoyed this moment. I could hear Angela's words she would say to me at almost every therapy session: Live in the moment, don't look at the past, and don't worry about the future. Just be in the moment. Even though he was staring at me, eagerly awaiting my verdict, we were having something that felt entirely foreign to me: we were having fun.

"I don't know if I've eaten a muffin that has this consistency. What's the secret ingredient?" I asked.

"I just can't give away Grandma's secret to just anyone, you know," he teased.

I smiled.

The kitchen smelled of a mix of cinnamon, baked goods, and morning all rolled into one. By the time John was done with his creations, it was nearly eleven, and I tried to stifle my yawn. He was washing the dishes and I was drying and putting things away.

"Did you ever think about becoming a chef?" I asked him.

"Many times," he said.

"So, what brought you here to the Inn?"

"Long story, I'm afraid," he said.

"I'd like to hear it if you want to share," I offered.

He sat down and cracked open a beer, leaving the solid, black apron he was wearing on the chair behind him. I hung the towel on the rack and sat across from him. I noticed his piercing hazel eyes—with flecks of green in them—for the first time. There was an intensity regarding the way he looked at that moment: serious and melancholy. But he didn't prevent the expression around his eyes to detract from the little smile that ran across his face. There were little fine lines around the corners of his eyes, and his skin looked a little sunburned around his nose and at the top of his cheekbones, probably from being outside in the sun when he was working in the yard. But it was when he got closer to me that I noticed how he smelled. He smelled freshly showered and clean, and I could detect the scent of cologne or aftershave on his skin. I'd almost forgotten what a man smelled like after two and a half years of not being around one.

"I went to the Air Force Academy because I always wanted to fly planes. It was my dream; I loved being up in the air ever since my parents took me on my first flight to Disney World as a kid, and I pursued it. I was pretty intense when it came to school and the academy, and I did well. When I graduated, I flew C-130 planes for the Air Force for nearly eight years, mostly cargo planes and special mission trips. I was deployed once, and it was a long year. When I left, I'd been in a three-year relationship. At the end of my deployment, I came home, and my girlfriend announced that she was going to marry someone else. I quit the military, got a job as a pilot trainer for Boeing, and did that for three years. After that stint, I decided to completely revamp my life," he said. "That's when I made the decision to move back to the Eastern Shore."

He paused momentarily, allowing me to digest the story.

"I'm sorry about that," I said. "I knew you were in the military, but had no idea you were a pilot. My parents never told me. And I'm sorry about what happened to your relationship."

"Don't be. I'm good. Looking back, the relationship wasn't a healthy one. I'm glad to be done with it all. It's amazing what can happen when you take stress away from your life and just simplify."

"I can imagine," I said. "You served your country. That's a lot of responsibility."

"Yes," he said. "It was."

"So, you moved home and…?" I paused so he could complete the sentence. I wanted to hear the rest of the story—the part about how he actually landed here at the Inn.

"It was my grandmother, actually. When I came home, I was staying with my parents for a few weeks trying to decide what my next course of action was going to be. I was strolling through the gardens at the retirement home with my grandmother when she told me about the 'lovely lady from Inn Significant who comes to play cards once a week.' Your mother mentioned to the group of ladies that there was a job open at the Inn. I called your mother, went to meet both your mom and dad, and that was it. They hired me on the spot. And the best part was that the cottage was part of the agreement, and I could live on the grounds."

"So, you are enjoying this way of life? Do you miss any of it?"

"You know, it's funny. Not one bit, actually. But I did get one good thing out of my prior careers," he said.

"What's that?"

"It's docked at the Yacht Club."

"Oh, nice," I said. "You went from being the captain of a plane to being the captain of a boat. I think I like the latter better, anyway. I'll have to take a peek at her sometime."

"Better yet," he said, "She and I will have to take you for a ride."

He smirked at me, testing me to see how I would respond to that offer.

"Is there any way we can get Karen to start sooner?" I asked.

CHAPTER 5

I had the dream again. The one where Gil and I are on the top of a beach cliff and we're walking and laughing and having a good time, and then he catches the edge of the rock, it gives, and he begins to fall. I reach for his hand, and I can't quite catch him. I hear his screams as he vanishes down into the surf.

I sat up, panting and sweating. It was six-thirty in the morning, and I tried to shake the vivid image from my mind. I got up and poured myself a glass of water. My heart was racing. The dream was a recurring one that haunted me every so often, and I couldn't put my finger on why it insisted on replaying over and over in my subconscious mind. Of course, my therapist had her own professional opinion about it.

My therapist. I decided I would call Angela today to see if she could recommend someone here in the Easton area. Therapy had been great for me, and I still believed I could use counseling. There was something so refreshing about speaking to someone who was completely unbiased about your life.

I crawled back into the bed and recounted what happened the night before. I'd spent the evening watching a guy—a man—bake muffins, while the two of us enjoyed amiable conversation. After we both cleaned up the kitchen and packaged some of the muffins in plastic containers for the Oxford Market to sell with the Inn's label on them, John and I walked back to our cottages together, said goodnight, and parted ways.

To distract myself, I grabbed paper and a pen, and made a list of things I needed to do. I wanted to take a ride into Easton and pick up a couple of new dresses at one of the boutiques to wear here for work. I also needed to pick up items from the grocery store.

At some point, I must have fallen back to sleep. When I awoke to the bright light coming through my blinds, I got up and showered so that I could help Colette in the kitchen with breakfast. I was eager to get to work. In the back of my mind, I could hear my mother saying she needed me to do this, to help them. It gave me a sense of purpose that I hadn't had in a long time.

But before I walked out the door and began my work day, I opened the little brown bag I carried back to the cottage last night, switched on the Keurig, and enjoyed John's muffin on the outdoor patio of the cottage as the light of the morning sun warmed me from the outside in.

*

At eight, I walked through the door of the Inn ready to help Colette distribute the food. I had set the tables in the dining room the night before. We served breakfast from eight-thirty until ten-thirty in the morning, and when I arrived, there was a man standing in the foyer wearing cargo pants and a graphic t-shirt with a brown, leather briefcase across his body. I'd heard those things referred to as man purses, which always made me giggle. His sunglasses were propped on the top of his head, and he had a rich suntan. He had messy, dark brown hair with traces of a receding hairline, and he stood with an erect posture, one that exuded confidence.

"May I help you?" I asked.

"Are you Emilia?" he asked me.

"Yes—Milly," I said.

"Right," he said. "I feel as if I know you already. My name is Miles Channing. I've known your mom and dad for years. How are they?"

We shook hands.

"They are well—in Ireland," I said.

"Wonderful. Good for them," he said. "I was wondering if you might have a room for me for the night. Had I known I would be back so soon, I would have made a reservation, but I tend to be spontaneous."

I checked the books, and we had one room available, the King Room, with a private porch and a view overlooking the water. When I began to tell him, he interrupted.

"I love that room. Perfect. Yes. Please book me for the night."

"Okay," I said. "You must be a frequent guest if you are familiar with the rooms."

"Yes. I'm in the process of writing a book about the Eastern Shore."

My eyes lit up, and he could tell by my expression that I was impressed. I started to get the paperwork together, and he handed me his credit card for payment. As I was processing the card, Colette walked into the room with a plate of scones on her way to the dining room.

"Oh," she exclaimed. "Good to see you, Mr. Channing!" she said.

He walked over to her and gave her a little squeeze around her arms and a peck on her cheek. "Good to see you, Colette. And please! Stop calling me Mr. Channing! Miles will do just fine."

I could see Colette blush just a little bit, flattered by the attention Miles was paying her.

"You know this is Milly, Lisa and Greg's daughter. She's taking over for the year while they are helping a friend in Ireland start up his own bed & breakfast."

"Yes," Miles said. "Lisa told me she was hopeful her daughter would pinch hit for them. We just met, although, I must admit, I feel as if I know her already from her mother."

It made me wonder what my mother had relayed to him. Did he know about Gil? My debilitating depression? My inability to cope with anything for the last two and a half years? My state of non-existence?

"I know she writes a bit, so we've got that in common," he said, still speaking to Colette, noting I was in the room, but talking around me a bit.

"I haven't written anything in a long time, but I always enjoy hearing what other writers are up to. Your book sounds interesting. Is there a particular focus?"

"I'm interested in the folklore, the stories people have from years on the Eastern Shore. There are plenty of straightforward history books, but I wanted to come at it from a different perspective and relay stories I hear from interviews with people that have been passed down for generations. The research is taking me a lot longer than I expected, which is why I'm here for, oh, I don't know, the umpteenth time."

"We love having you," Colette said.

Miles pointed to Colette and said to me, "See? That's why I keep coming back."

"So, then," Colette began, flirting with him a little, "you can sit and enjoy breakfast which will be fully done in about ten minutes. Newspapers are on the huntboard."

"Sounds perfect," he said, finding a spot near the window, beams of sunshine cascading through it illuminating his table. He poured himself a cup of black coffee, opened up his choice of newspaper, and sat back and relaxed.

*

When Angela finally answered her phone around noon, she was happy to give me the name of someone nearby, but at the same time, she did her best to boost my confidence that I was on the path to moving on…that the worst stages of grieving were almost over.

"I understand," I said. "I'd just like the number of a therapist here just in case."

"I think you're going to be okay, Milly," she said to me. "You know how to cope. We've been over this a hundred times. Remember when you told me your mother wanted you to run the Inn? Deep inside and quietly, I cheered. This was exactly the type of situation that could help you heal from all that pain. It's okay to live a little. Would Gil really have wanted you to be sad for another year? You've been sad and mourned for a long time now. It's okay to have fun. It's okay to hang out with a guy and make muffins. It's okay to feel a sense of purpose. These feelings are all normal, and you should not harbor any guilt about any of it."

I sighed. She was right, of course, but I'd been dependent on sharing my thoughts and feelings with her for over two years. Letting go of that ability was scary to me. I still needed someone to hear what I was thinking.

"Do you want to see a man or a woman?" she asked.

I paused, noticing I was pacing back and forth in the living room of the cottage. I had the windows open, allowing the air to blow through, and the curtains were gently moving in the breeze. Both fans were on, circulating the air. I was perspiring, not from the heat, but from the conversation.

Finally, I spoke. "You know what? Let me give this a try for another couple of weeks. Then, if I need to talk to someone, I'll call you back. You are right—and I hate to tell you that because you love to hear me say you are right—but I think you've given me some great coping skills. I've been useless for so long, it feels uncomfortable to be undoing that."

"Right. We need to break that uselessness habit. Look at you! Three days, and listen to yourself. You sound pretty healthy to me. Call me in a week. We'll touch base. If you want to set up phone times to talk, we can. It's billed the same way."

"I think I've made you rich enough," I said.

She laughed. And then, so did I.

*

John didn't mind at all when I asked if he would cover for me while I shopped in Easton. I hurried back to the cottage to change. I wore shorts, a t-shirt, and sneakers, and put my hair in a ponytail. I looked at myself in the mirror. There were lines on my face that weren't there before, but at the age of thirty-seven, what did I expect? I would soon be thirty-eight, and those certainly weren't laugh lines. It's funny how the way you see yourself in a mirror isn't at all what the camera sees. When I had to renew my driver's license and I saw the picture the man took, I almost didn't recognize myself. The woman in the photo looked unbearably pathetic and glum. My mother was not inaccurate in her description of me: prior to Gil's death, I was what some might call an unusually happy person.

But what did anyone expect when the love of your life dies suddenly and you end up passed out on the floor from the news? He was the man I loved wholeheartedly—the man I thought I was going to grow old with and pamper grandchildren with as we rocked on our front porch in some southern town overlooking a river. And then, to also lose a baby, the one we made together, the one that would have allowed me to have a connection to him. The thought of my losses still made me shiver.

I shook my head, trying to shake away the memories, put Burt's Bees on my lips, grabbed my keys, and exited the cottage. Tears would have to wait until later. I had a little ride to take, and I was looking forward to rolling down the windows, feeling the wind in my hair, and doing a little shopping. I tossed my purse in the car.

"Enjoy," John called to me as he was tending to the garden.

"Thanks," I yelled back, ready to tackle the shopping spree in Easton.

I parked on Goldsborough Street and got a spot right in front of Dragonfly Boutique; it was nestled among other stores in a red, brick building with crisp, white trimmed windows full of its best items, including dresses and accessories. The front door was propped wide open, and I walked inside. It smelled fresh and new, like unworn fabric and lavender, and the woman behind the counter, who looked to be my age, called "hello" to me.

"Hello," I said back.

"Can I help you find anything?" she asked.

"Just looking for a couple of new summer dresses," I said. The clothes I owned didn't fit properly now. During the aftermath of Gil's death, I swore off eating and lost so much weight that people became concerned. That was when my mother got involved and decided therapy was needed. It was perhaps part of the culmination of my biggest meltdown—the day after I threw the dishes against the wall, she saw me change out of my nightgown and into sweat pants, she noticed just how thin I had become, and within hours I was sitting in front of Angela for my first session.

"Dresses are all over the store. Let me know if you want to try anything on or need help with sizes."

"Thank you," I responded. I was the only person in the store, and I took my time browsing. There was music on—some eighties station—and an oldie by Culture Club played in the background. I spotted a turquoise dress with flowers at the neckline. It was very different than anything I had, and the color reminded me of a Tiffany's box. I pulled that one off the rack, along with a blue and white dress with red piping. In the back, I browsed the rack and found an all black, simple dress with ruffles at the sweetheart neckline.

"May I try these on?" I asked the woman.

"Of course," she said. "Are you new to town? I'm Tillie."

"Nice to meet you. I'm Milly. We rhyme."

"Funny," she said. "Where do you live?"

"My mother and father own Inn Significant in Oxford, and I'm here for a year while they are away."

"Oh!" she exclaimed. "Very cool."

"Thank you."

"Your mother knows my mother. I think they work the annual flower show together. I was sorry to hear about the death of your husband."

"Thank you," I said, trying not to have to discuss Gil. "Do you own this store?"

"No, I just work here part time. My friend owns it." She studied my three items. "Those are some good picks," she said, and led me to the dressing room.

Within minutes, I was paying her for all three. There's quiet satisfaction that comes from buying new pieces of clothing. It's refreshing. Out with the old, and in with the new, at least that's what I kept telling myself.

As she handed me the bag, she thanked me again for coming in, and said,

"Is John still working at the Inn?" she asked.

"He is," I said, a little stunned that she knew him by name.

"It's too bad about what happened to him, but I think he likes working there."

"How do you know John?"

"We went to high school together. I've run into him a couple of times since he's been back."

"Well, he's very helpful at the Inn, that's for sure," I said. "As a matter of fact, I have to get back to my afternoon duties. Have a great day."

I got outside and tossed my package through the open back window of the car. I needed some air because Tillie was spoiling my shopping experience by bringing up Gil and whatever John had chosen not to tell me. She obviously knew something about him that

I did not. It made me wonder what he was keeping from me that he didn't want to share.

I began the short trek back to the Inn and appreciated that I understood one thing better than most people did about life: we've all experienced something we'd rather not discuss or remember.

CHAPTER 6

The Tred Avon River was incredibly serene early that evening. I wiped down the Adirondack chairs that were positioned along the water on the lawn so the guests could enjoy them at night or in the morning. Most of our guests were still lingering on the porch after the four o'clock tea. John and I had cleaned up most of it, and he was at the office desk assisting people with their dinner reservations, which gave me the opportunity to be outside.

An osprey soared by with twigs in his beak. His massive wings were spread out as he glided through the air, carrying those twigs to a piling where he was building a large nest. Ospreys were a pride of the Chesapeake Bay, and made their homes in the region from spring through the end of summer, before they headed farther south for the winter months. They were impressive birds, and I loved observing them and learning about them when I was younger from my grandfather as we often used binoculars to see them clearly. My grandfather had also bought me a book about birds when I was in school to help me write a book report on them.

I stood in awe of the scenery that surrounded me and remembered running around this place when it belonged to my grandparents. Barefoot on the lawn and feeling the grass between my toes, I would run around calling to the birds—chasing them sometimes—and always jealous of their ability to fly and soar. My grandfather would tell me stories about the river, probably invented stories loosely based on history, which typically involved the captain of a ship and his ability to survive the high seas. As I turned to look at the Inn from the shore, I wondered if my grandfather would recognize this place now. While the land was the same, the house and additional buildings were so very different from what they looked like when the property was not a business but simply a home.

"Hey, Milly," a voice was calling to me as he walked down the lawn over to me.

"Hi, Miles," I said. "Have you had a nice day?"

"I have, thanks. I'm tired now. I think I just interviewed the most intriguing fellow to date. He had so many stories to tell me about his great-grandfather's tobacco farm, that I'm almost wondering if I should be writing fiction instead of a collection of narratives. It makes you wonder how much is embellished and how much is actually true. The guy was so animated. Whew. I think I may need a beer."

He sat down in the Adirondack chair I had cleaned, and asked me to join him for a moment. I enjoyed talking with the guests; it was typically innocuous, so I never minded.

"So how are you enjoying being here?" he asked.

"So far, so good. I mean, how can you not appreciate this beauty all around you? There are worse places I could be, right?"

"Exactly," he said. "That's why I write about things that allow me to travel. I like to see what the world has to offer."

I liked the way he said that: what the world has to offer. I'd been pretty mad at the world for a while, and that hadn't gotten me anywhere but holed up in a therapist's office rehashing the gruesome details of what my life had become. Breathing this air, feeling the openness of the land and the water—on day three—this was exactly the kind of therapy that might actually have a chance of working.

"So, where should I go for dinner, what should I eat, and would you like to join me?"

*

We decided to go casual, and Miles was in the mood for oysters, so we drove the nine miles to Easton and got a table without waiting at Washington Street Pub & Oyster Bar. We were seated in the right back corner of the pub that boasted brick walls and a tin ceiling. The Friday crowd was starting to build. Miles ordered a dark beer by Heavy Seas, and I had a glass of the house Pinot Grigio. We raised our glasses in a toast to Easton.

"I don't know…there's something about life on the Eastern Shore. It's just so relaxing and the people are kind and genuine. You don't find that everywhere—and I get around."

"I get that impression," I said, teasing him.

"No, not in that way," he laughed, running his hand through his hair. "It's just that travel writing has kept me moving a lot over the last ten years or so. I think it's starting to show in my face. I'm noticing more lines when I look at myself in the mirror."

"Funny you should say that," I said. "I noticed the same thing earlier today. Only on men, the aging looks distinguished, and on women, it just makes us look old and tired."

"Trust me. You don't look old. And you don't appear to be tired."

"I'll just say 'thank you' and leave it at that." I smiled. It was a nice compliment to receive.

"The dress is nice, too. Great color."

"Thanks," I said. "I just got it today from a boutique around the corner."

"In the bustling mecca of Easton?"

"That's right," I said. "Don't knock it."

"I'm not! You just heard me say minutes ago how much I loved it here."

He was easy to talk to; he made you feel as if you'd been friends your whole lives. Conversation with him was not work; it was just comfortable. I watched him use that same gift this morning when he was flirting with Colette, who obviously didn't mind it at all. Of course, I'd basically been living in solitude since Gil's death and the loss of the baby, so it was delightfully refreshing to observe someone who made conversation and friendships seem effortless.

"So, tell me why you stopped writing."

I looked at him for a moment and didn't hesitate. "My husband, Gil, died in a car accident involving a tractor trailer, and weeks prior, I had lost a baby at the end of my first trimester. I didn't have the drive to write, take a shower, get dressed, eat, or talk to people, and I gave up my job writing features for a magazine in Washington, D.C. Just stopped altogether. Basically, I extinguished my own writing career."

Miles remained quiet. I think he expected that there was more to come after that litany. But there wasn't. I said it. There it was—the story in a nutshell.

"Jeez," he said. "That's just all so tragic. How long were you married?"

"Ten years, but I'd been with him for fifteen."

"Love of your life?" he asked sweetly.

"Love of my life."

Miles raised his beer to me. "To Gil," he said.

I clinked his glass. "To Gil," I said, swallowing hard. "Now, let's talk about something else. I don't want to get mired down in misery in front of you. Tell me about the tobacco farmer full of tall tales."

*

Miles had a strong physique, and it made me wonder how he kept in such good physical condition despite all the traveling and restaurant eating he was required to do. His book deal was his first; after years of writing travel pieces, he pitched the idea of a folklore book about the Eastern Shore of Maryland to several publishers, and finally, he got a bite. He drafted his first half of the book, and he was working on the second half, still maintaining his demanding travel schedule in between writing chapters of the book. The tobacco farmer was definitely an entertaining and lively character, and Miles relayed several stories over the course of the dinner, including one that involved him protesting against President Bill Clinton's proposed increase of tobacco farm taxes back in the nineties.

"The guy's kind of a maniac, but the farm's been in his family for generations, so I understand his passion. Want a cigarette?" Miles said, mockingly reaching for his back pocket.

"Hilarious," I said.

"Your own writing career doesn't have to be over, you know," he said, eyebrows raised.

I shrugged. "Maybe not," I agreed.

"In fact, I know of a writing job that involves Inn Significant directly."

"What's that?" I asked, as he had piqued my curiosity.

"Your website could use some serious love. Have you seen it? It needs new photographs, better quotes from guests, maybe even a beautifully written overview, information about the proprietors— your family—that sounds better than what is there. Have you ever thought about blogging from the Inn? Might be pretty good stuff."

"I'll have to investigate later," I said. "I haven't paid much attention to it."

"You could do so much more with it. Maybe you could even hire a college kid to help revamp it. Set up some social media."

It was an interesting idea, and one that I promised to consider. When our plates were cleared and Miles generously paid the bill, we were left with the remainder of our drinks. I thanked him for taking me out and for being so gracious, and I needed to be sure to thank John for covering. The place was full now, and the volume in the pub grew louder.

"I'm glad we got to meet, Milly. Your mother has always spoken so highly of you. And of course, you know how much she loves you."

"I do. She was my saving grace," I said. "Let's just hope I can take care of the Inn and not send it into ruin in my parents' absence."

"It seems to be doing just fine," he said. "In fact, if I want to stay another night, is there a room available or are you all booked?"

"We can check when we get back."

As we walked out of the pub, I noticed that a few women looked up to admire my dress. It was either that, or they were admiring the man who was walking just slightly behind me, allowing me pass through the narrow bar area first.

Chapter 7

The next morning, I was up early and sat on my deck with the umbrella open, sipping my coffee as I opened my laptop. The poor thing was dusty from two years of negligible care and lack of use. I had charged it when I got back from dinner last night, and it powered up and began working just as it should. I was perusing Inn Significant's website, something my parents set up and hired an independent consultant to manage. Clearly, they didn't renew the contract. Miles was right; the site hadn't been updated in what appeared to be a year.

I scrolled through the site—there were photographs that needed retaking, verbiage that wasn't strong or descriptive, dated material that needed rewriting, and a general lack of compelling storytelling through both pictures and words that pervaded every page. If I decided to tackle this project, I would have my work cut out for me. It would have to be rebuilt from scratch.

It was seven o'clock in the morning. My sister would be awake. With a child who was a terrible sleeper, she'd probably been up for hours. She picked up the phone on the second ring.

"Hey," she said.

"How are you?"

"Tired. Always tired," she moaned, as she let out a yawn.

"The bigger question is how are you? How's the Inn?"

"So far, it's good. It's like stepping into another world; the pace is so slow here, but I'm not minding it at all. Don't be jealous. Mom and Dad bought me a pink bike."

"One of those beach cruisers with a pretty wicker basket?"

"Yes," I said.

"Not fair, Mills. You always got the good stuff, and I always wanted a pink bike!"

"The benefits of being the first-born, I suppose."

I could hear Gracie chuckle under her tired breath. I continued. "So, I'm calling with a proposition. I know you've been home for a year with Abbie, and the last thing you want to do is start a project, but could you coach me through the technical side of fixing the Inn's website? It looks horrible."

"I've been telling Mom that for a while, but she didn't want to offend the woman who built it for her. I think she closed her business, though."

"So, that's a yes? You could help me set up a new site for them?"

Before my sister had the baby, she worked for a small advertising firm in Philadelphia, and I knew she collaborated with a colleague to help reformat a couple of websites. It wasn't her primary role, but I remembered her showing me one she had revamped a few years ago, and it was better than average.

"That's a yes. Are you rewriting it?"

"I think I will. And I'll dust off my Nikon and take some new improved photos of the place. The old ones look so dated."

"You were always good at that," Gracie said. "I should have you take some pictures of Abbie by the water. I have a few empty frames around the house."

"I'd love to. Come and visit me. I'd like to see my niece. Mom said you would."

"I will," she said. "Maybe next month when Cal goes out of town."

"Road trip," I said. "Sounds good. How are things with Cal?"

"Better. I think we're finally getting back on track. I used to watch those afternoon talk shows and think 'where do women find these losers who can't cope with family life?' until I experienced it myself. Work is less busy for him now, and Cal's coming around to our new lifestyle with a child. He doesn't miss weekends with the boys as much now that some of his friends are having kids, too. I'm seeing big improvements. Plus, I think now that both of us are getting some sleep it is helping a lot."

"I'm glad to hear it," I said. "I was a little worried about you two."

"No worries now. We're just fine."

"Good. I'm happy for you," I said.

"Thanks."

"So, I'm going to get started on this project, and then we'll get this thing moving. Check your schedule to see if you can come down and spend some time with me. We can surprise Mom and Dad with a new, improved website."

"Milly, can I tell you something?" Gracie asked.

"Sure."

"You sound better."

*

Colette outdid herself in the kitchen that weekend. The stuffed French toast was a hit, and the berries and cream were so fresh. We even took the time to squeeze fresh orange juice. Colette and I talked about trying to revive the garden on the side of the property, and despite John's tentative response when we both excitedly started mapping out the plans, which included lettuce, cucumbers, fresh herbs, and pepper and tomato plants, he promised to have a good attitude, if not a perfectly green thumb.

"Nothing ventured, nothing gained," Colette said. "It will be a thing of beauty. And just think, John, you'll get to eat the stuff we grow. Besides, it's still May, and we've got all summer to coax this thing along."

We were sitting at the small farm table in the cook's kitch-en—the main kitchen, which was closed off to the guests—the same table where John and I sat the other night and made muffins. We were snacking on the breakfast while guests ate in the main dining room, having already refilled everything they needed on the hunt-board.

"So, how was dinner last night with Miles?" Colette asked.

"Let me guess. Miles told you," I said.

She winked.

"It was good," I said.

I had no interest in discussing it at all. John knew I went to dinner with Miles, and although I didn't know John well, I knew him just enough to know that he wasn't the prying type or one prone to gossip. Colette, on the other hand…

"What did you guys talk about?"

"Mostly his writing, his book, and the tobacco farmer he's been interviewing who seems to be a real piece of work," I said, try-ing to keep it light. "I have to say, it was nice to talk to a fellow writer, even though I gave it up."

"We'll see about that," Colette said.

I laughed. John looked up from his plate, as I began to talk. "Actually, he had a good idea for the Inn. He mentioned to me how our website could use some attention, so I may put my writer's hat back on for a bit and see if I can spruce it up a little," I said. "And, if you see me with my Nikon walking around, you'll know what I'm up to."

"Now that sounds like a brilliant idea," Colette said. "Have you told your parents?"

"Let's not," I said. "I want it to be a surprise. And I'm going to work on the design of it with my sister. She has some experience with revamping websites."

"You could blog about the Inn, too," John said.

"Funny," I said. "That's exactly what Miles suggested."

*

Yesterday, John and I tucked the mountain bike into the garage, and I promised him I would take my new one out for a spin. It was Saturday, and I had an hour free in the afternoon for my exercise. Oxford isn't a big town, but I had yet to ride around, so I decided to take the pink beach cruiser for a test drive. I loved the little bicycle and the sentiment from my parents; the color of it and the wicker basket actually made me happy.

People always use the expression, "it's like riding a bike; you just get back up and ride again," to describe people who have fallen off or have fallen away from something. My fanny hadn't been on a bike since Gil died. In fact, there was a lot I hadn't done since Gil died. God, I missed him. I still missed him morning, afternoon, and night, especially at night, when I had to crawl inside the cool sheets without the warmth of his body beside me. I missed his sweet kisses and the way he romanced me in the bedroom, always tender, always loving. I missed the way his hands felt on the small of my back and the way the crook of his neck smelled. I missed that I couldn't tell him about a movie I watched, a book I read, or something funny my sister said. After a little over ten years of marriage, he was here one day and gone the next. I wanted to tell him how unfair that was to both of us. How a person's accidental death left no time for last goodbyes and one more meaningful 'I love you'. Why was his life cut so short and mine left so unbearable because of an accident in the rain?

And yet, here I was trying to persevere. I was on a pink bike with a basket in a place as picturesque as it could be and I hadn't cried in two days. It was a miracle. I'd come close to tears several times, but the waterworks did not turn on. Perhaps I am dried up—all out of tears because they'd been exhausted over time. Or perhaps that was just wishful thinking.

Enough. I didn't want to think this deeply while I was riding. Be in the moment. All I had to do was focus on riding and looking at the houses, the water, and the general scenery.

Several properties were for sale, some more expensive than others. I knew the real estate in Oxford could be expensive, and I could only imagine what the Inn would go for if it sold today. Thank goodness it was not an option, but I did often wonder how long my parents would want to maintain it and keep it going. I turned down one street, then another, listening to my wheels as I pedaled along. When I was straightening out the magazines and brochures earlier, I noticed an article about Scottish Highland Creamery on Tilghman Street, an ice cream parlor that was voted Best on the Eastern Shore and ranked as number five in the nation by a top-notch travel site. My wallet was in the basket, just in case I decided to sample the goods.

I parked my bike in front of the Creamery, along with many other people, and decided to give it a try. My Italian heritage must have been speaking to me, because I chose one of the day's specials: the Tiramisu cone. The Creamery sits along the water on the dock. Since it was another spectacular day, I sat and enjoyed the view—and my cone.

"Didn't I just help you?" the woman behind the counter asked teasingly when I went back up to the counter.

"Yes, but I'm back. For my friend, of course. Can I get a pint of that Tiramisu to take home?"

I caught myself as I said it. I had just used the word "home" to describe the Inn.

*

I knocked on the door to John's cottage, and he opened it.

"Hey," he said, as he stepped out onto his front porch, and closed the door behind him. "I was just about to go to the office and check on things."

"Not before you put this in your freezer," I said, presenting him with the pint I had hidden behind my back.

"I see you went to the Creamery."

"Tiramisu—you like?"

"Love it, actually. Thank you."

"You're welcome."

"How was the bike? Any kinks in it?"

"It was just perfect," I said. And I meant it.

*

That evening, the clouds blew in, and rain was predicted to last through the night. I didn't want to spend time in the cottage alone, so I slipped into my rain boots, opened my umbrella, and walked over to the Inn, settling myself in the parlor. The bookshelves were filled with all my mother's favorite novels and nonfiction works. As a high school English teacher for many years, my mother instilled the love of reading in me, always doing her best to guide me to books she thought I would like. That wasn't to say that she didn't challenge me to read things that might not be my favorite genre; every once in a while, I took a leap of faith and read a book I wouldn't normally pick up myself. It was my mother's incredible love for both reading and the English language that propelled me to study journalism in college. I knew I didn't want to study the classics or be an English teacher, but rather become a writer of mainstream, everyday things.

When I secured an internship at a local newspaper, the section editor put me on the local events beat, and I began to build a portfolio of published articles. Writing pieces about people and places was enjoyable for me; I loved digging into stories and then watching them unfold in my own words. When a colleague told me about the opening at *Washingtonian Magazine*, I sent my clips, and although the process took more than two months altogether, I ended up getting the job. I wrote feature stories for the magazine for years, talked to kids in schools for career days, and sat on a couple of writers' groups in the Maryland, Virginia, and the Washington metropolitan area. I never grew tired of seeing my byline. It was always a thrill.

I'm certain Gil would have been tremendously disappointed that I stopped writing when he stopped living. He would have grilled me about my emotional decision, and sometimes I could hear his voice in my head. *Did you forget how much you love it? Have you forgotten how good you are at building a story? Why have you allowed yourself to let go of something you are so passionate about, Milly?* Because you died, I would tell him. Because when you stopped living, I started dying.

My editor called and called the house, practically begging me to return. "I've got a great story for you to cover, Mills," she would say. "It's perfect for you." When I had to explain to her for the twentieth time that I simply couldn't write anymore—that it wasn't just writer's block and that I actually had lost the will to write—she finally gave up on me, and that was that. People can only be expected to be patient for so long.

Scanning the shelves, I came across my mother's prized possessions: her leather bound, full set of Jane Austen novels. I remembered she paid a fortune for those copies, and here they sat on a shelf in the parlor of her Inn for anyone to see, read, touch, and borrow; she was very trusting, my mother, yet she never was worried that these books might wander away from the Inn.

"I see you like Jane Austen."

"Oh, good evening, Ms. Simons," I said. "Is everything okay?"

"Just fine, dear," she said. "I guess you and I had the same idea for the evening."

"Great minds think alike," I said.

Ms. Simons was a guest from England with an eloquent accent who was visiting with her sister, Rosamunde. They attended an afternoon wedding in Easton and returned earlier. Luckily, the wedding took place while the weather was glorious—and a tent on the water provided shade from the sun. Ms. Simons was in loungewear now, having ditched her dress and low pumps she wore to the wedding.

"Your mother has sensible and charming decorating taste," she said. "I love everything about this place. All the white everywhere has me feeling comfortable and peaceful. It's just so relaxing."

"I will tell her you said so."

"Oh, I have told her many times myself. We were here last year for the elaborate engagement party. My cousins like to do things big."

"Well, we are so happy you chose to come back and stay with us again," I said.

"Rosamunde and I decided to extend this trip. We didn't do that last time. Tomorrow, we shall venture off to Washington, D.C. for two nights, then we board the train to Philadelphia and New York. We won't be back in England for twelve more days. This may be the longest trip we've ever taken together."

"It's nice that you and your sister enjoy traveling together."

"Yes, we get on quite well, actually. Have you got any siblings?"

"Yes," I said. "I have a sister, Gracie, who claims she will visit next month. She lives just outside Philadelphia. She's the mother of my darling niece, Abbie."

"That's lovely," she said. "My sister has children, but I've never married, so no children in my life."

"None in mine either," I said, "not by my choice."

"Does your husband not want to have children?" she asked.

"I'm not married," I said. "My husband died two and a half years ago in a car accident."

Ms. Simons became still and embarrassed. "Oh, dear. I'm terribly sorry. I shouldn't have pried the way I did."

"It's okay, Ms. Simons. It's getting easier to say it, I think. I can't swear to it, though," I said. She was a sweet lady, and she put me right at ease. Plus, tomorrow morning, she would be gone, and I might never see her again, so I took comfort and blurted out the rest of the story. "I lost a baby just three weeks prior to the accident. So, you could say, I had a double whammy."

"My dear. Indeed, you have had a double whammy."

She moved closer to me and she motioned me to sit. There

was something about her posture, her movement, the kindness that exuded from every pore in her being, and the warmth that emanated from her eyes that made me sit and listen to what she was about to tell me.

"Since it's just the two of us here, I'm going to tell you a short story, if you will permit me to do so. Don't let the word 'regret' become a part of your vocabulary, and here's what I mean. I am unmarried. My fellow—a wonderful darling of a man—became ill when we were engaged. I loved him with all of my heart, dear. He was the most special man in the world to me. His illness, a rare form of cancer, took his life before we could even begin a life together. After his death, I couldn't look at another man because no one could ever measure up to my Martin. I was angry. My sister even stopped speaking to me for a spell. No one could get through to me. I blamed the universe, God, my family, fate…you name it…and I was a bitter woman for many, many years. People tried to pair me with other men, and there were many blind dates, but I simply could not move on. And now, look at me. I'm in my late fifties, and I am alone. This isn't the life I would have chosen for myself. My sister has been sweet and become my best companion, but she has her own family and a husband to look after. Keep your heart open, even when all you want to do is lock it up," she said. "There's so much I regret now."

I found myself reaching for a tissue, as the tears began to

build and then drip. I guess my days of crying were not completely over. My heart ached for her, for me, for Martin, for Gil, for lost time, for regret, for a lost love, and for the bond that just formed within minutes in this congenial parlor in Inn Significant.

Ms. Simons wiped away the tear on my cheek. "You are still young, beautiful, and lovely, with many years ahead of you. Don't do what I did and perch yourself in a nest of negativity."

"Thank you, Ms. Simons," I said.

"Gretel," she said. "Please call me Gretel."

"Thank you, Gretel," I said.

"And when all else fails, memorize Winston Churchill's greatest quote and recite it to yourself and believe it. Do you know it? It goes like this: 'May the pain you have known and the conflict you have experienced give you the strength to walk through life facing each new situation with courage and optimism.' Frankly, I wish I'd paid more attention to it myself. There's a lot to be said for living life full of optimism."

"I will," I said. "And it's not too late for you, either."

The words lingered as we sat there in silence for moments, pensive, each of us alone with our thoughts, but together listening to the rain as it tickled the awnings, bounced off the roof, and breathed life back into everything that was the landscape and the makeup of the Inn.

Chapter 8

Miles stayed at the Inn an additional night, but I didn't see him the day after our dinner at all. He was busy conducting interviews all day, and he must have come back to the Inn after my chat with Gretel. I was up early the next morning, knowing I had to meet Karen at the office on her first day. Miles was putting his bag into his car, which was parked adjacent to the office.

"Good morning!" he said, cheerfully.

"Good morning to you," I said. "You must have been busy yesterday. I didn't see you at all."

"I was. Three interviews in a row lined up, and the final one invited me to dinner at the local pub, where I got to talk to a whole bunch of interesting folks. I have a notebook full of notes, which I now have to dissect. It's a messy business this nonfiction book writing. There's so much to sort through."

"I can only imagine. Sounds cumbersome, but I'm sure you'll put a wonderful story together."

"Let's hope," he said.

"You're not staying for breakfast this morning?"

"No, I wish I could. I've got to go. I have an article due in the next week, and haven't even spent any time on it. But, I'll be back."

He had a cup of coffee in a disposable cup from the Inn in

his hand (my mother had ordered these with Inn Significant's name on them), and after he loaded the trunk of his car, he was ready to go. He reached for me and gave me a big hug goodbye.

"It was a pleasure, as always, staying here. I look forward to coming back soon. Next time, I plan to get a little recreation in—I want to rent one of those jet skis."

"You should," I said. "Thanks for coming, and for the inspiration. I've already started the website project…at least, I've started to get it organized."

"Good girl," he said, pleased that he convinced me that it was an idea worth pursuing. "I can't wait to see its transformation."

We both smiled at each other for a moment. I waved back to him as he drove his car down the gravel driveway and off the premises, his left hand out the window, waving goodbye.

Just as he turned the corner, I saw Karen approaching. She was walking from town, and I was so pleased to see her promptness that Monday morning. We ventured into the office, and John was up and ready to go as well. I seated myself at the pine desk, determined to take a peek at the books. I slated Mondays as my administrative day, where I would spend time paying bills and salaries and logging our data into the computer just as my father had taught me. John ran through information with Karen at the main desk, going over procedures step-by-step. Colette burst through the door with

a smile, croissants, strawberries, and a pitcher of fresh juice to welcome Karen on her first morning at the Inn.

"Three check-outs today and three check-ins. The summer
months are always the busiest, followed by the fall and spring. Winter can be much quieter, but we still manage to have guests coming and going…" I heard John explaining to her. Karen's expression
showed interest and respect; she was taking notes in a small journal
she brought with her, and I could tell she would be a quick study.

"Do we have bocce balls?" I blurted out, as I was trying to
imagine what other activities we could bring to the Inn.

"I haven't come across any," John answered. "But I think
there's a croquet set in the garage."

The lawn was expansive with a low roll to the river; I figured
it would be a good spot for our guests to play bocce. I could have
sworn my grandfather had an old set of bocce balls because I remembered distinctly playing with him on the freshly-cut grass when
I was younger. I made a note to call my parents later to see where
they might be. Of course, I could buy newer ones, but I thought the
older set added a bit of nostalgia to what was already charming.

After changing over a few rooms, throwing sheets and towels
into the wash, and getting our new arrivals registered in the afternoon, I unzipped the bag that housed my Nikon. The battery needed
charging, so I'd let the camera charge all night long. When I turned
it on, everything was in working order, and I was eager to take some

new shots of the Inn; I especially wanted to capture the moment the sun began to set in the afternoon, casting its light on the Inn's facade. I was pretty certain that whatever I shot as the sun set would be far better than what was already on the website.

The lighting in the late afternoon proved to be particularly good. I was able to photograph the Inn and its landscaping, including the roses that were in bloom. It was too early for the hydrangeas, but I expected them to blossom within the next few weeks. I aligned the Adirondack chairs and adjusted the pillows on them making sure they were appealing in the shot. I also wanted to capture the peacefulness of the screened-in porches that faced the water on both the upper and lower levels of the Inn.

"You know, we could take my boat out and you could shoot the Inn from the water," John said as he approached me on the lawn as I was working the camera, trying my best to get usable shots.

"That would be fantastic," I said. "Maybe next week after Karen becomes comfortable?"

"Sounds good," he said. "Tomorrow we tackle the garden? The food garden?"

"Okay," I said. He'd been calling it "the food garden" ever since Colette and I concocted the notion last week. He called it that in order to distinguish it from the other gardens on site that needed constant attention and upkeep. I actually found it funny. Over the last couple of days, he had cleared the area where the food garden would go and set it off with wood framing. "This way guests will know that what Colette may make them for breakfast or afternoon tea comes directly from here," he said when I complimented him and said he was making it more perfect than I expected. Something told me he was happy to have a new project. I couldn't resist teasing him, though.

"Yes. I think it's going to be amazing provided we don't kill everything in it."

"That's the sort of optimism we're looking for, Milly," he joked, punching me lightly on my arm.

I began to walk away to take more shots when I turned back and saw John standing there, hands on both hips, as he looked out across the river. His silhouette and the lighting were too perfect for me not to take the shot.

"That's not going on the website, right?" he said turning around as he heard the 'click.'

"One never knows," I said.

*

Tea was set on the porch for the afternoon, and Colette left for the day. Karen was busy in the office as well. I gave her a job to do in between her regular duties: surf websites and find examples with pretty and functional designs. I wanted to send my sister the links to some well-designed websites I thought might suit the Inn to give her a starting point, so between the two of us, I hoped to gather a collection for her to peruse.

I decided to spend some time in my cottage putting things away, and asked John if he could stop over in an hour to help me cart things I wouldn't need to the detached garage. In order to feel more comfortable, I needed to finish unpacking, stow empty containers and boxes away, and tuck my luggage away. All the windows were open in the cottage, and the breeze blowing off the water was free of humidity; it was lovely. I opened the French patio doors. The heat of summer would descend upon us, and before it grabbed hold, I wanted to enjoy the fresh, spring air.

The kitchen was in order, as I brought only the essentials with me: my Cuisinart, which was a particular favorite of mine for making all sorts of meals from breakfast to shakes; the non-stick griddle for pancakes and panini; and the drinking glasses I purchased from Crate & Barrel. My mother stocked the cottage well, so I knew I didn't need to unbox many other things other than those few that were special to me. The other boxes I labeled and would store in the garage. Of the four large suitcases I brought (two were mine; two were Gil's), only one was left to unload and put away in the dresser and closet, so I hopped to it.

When one lone box remained, I opened it. I must have forgotten to label it. Gil's belongings were inside the box. As soon as
I lifted the lid, an aroma I had been familiar with for fifteen years
wafted into the air, and I remembered all that I had saved. Gil's
favorite ballcap, the Orioles hat he bought at the ballpark when we
went with a group of friends to the game; his favorite t-shirt from
our trip to Italy; his college sweatshirt I seemed to wear more than
he did; his wallet made of Italian leather; several cards and letters I
wrote to him over the years; the Burberry watch I gave him on our
tenth anniversary. I picked up the shirt, the one I could picture him
in when I closed my eyes that said "Italia," and brought it to my nose.
He couldn't really be dead; there was still a scent of him in the clothing. His wallet contained a picture of the two of us. I sat down on
the floor of my parents' cottage wishing I'd never opened this box. I
wept uncontrollably, ignoring all the advice I'd received from Gretel,
Angela, my parents, my sister, and even Miles.

After many minutes of inhaling the scent of my dead husband and having a complete breakdown, I heard the knock at the
door.

*

He knocked twice, and then, when I didn't answer, he
knocked again, slowly opening the unlocked door. "Milly?" he called.

I sniffled, but couldn't speak, and he opened the door all the way to find me among a heap of belongings on the floor looking at him through damp and bloodshot eyes. He moved quickly over to me—my eyes glassy and my tears soaked with mascara—and squatted down beside me.

"Are you okay?" he asked.

"I just found a box of Gil's things," I said, trying to pull myself together. "I'm trying really hard to let go, and just when I was starting to feel a little better, I open a box full of memories." I wiped my tears with the back of my hand, and John got up and handed me the tissue from the side table.

"You've only been here a week," he said. "These things take time."

"It's already been two and a half years," I said.

"Well, some people need more time than others to mourn and cope with things. It's okay. You're doing great." He pressed his back up against the sofa doing his best to be comforting. "Life is hard sometimes, isn't it?"

"Yes," I sniffled.

"I think sometimes we just have to accept that life is hard, it's unfair, it's ironic, and it can be debilitating, but only if we let it be that way. There's still a lot of beauty in the world if we look for it."

The breeze caused the wind chimes to make music as the curtains blew in the breeze. He was right; I had only been at the Inn for a week, and yet, somehow it felt as if I'd been around for much longer, as if I'd known John for years, as if Colette and I were old friends, and as if I lived in Washington, D.C. months ago...years ago.

"I feel so ridiculous having you see me like this," I said. "What must you think of me?"

He picked up my hand and held it.

"That one's easy. I think you are a beautiful woman who has suffered a great loss in her life and is slowly coming back from years of hurt. I see that you have loved deeply and have lost deeply. But I also see resilience in you. And I think your family sees it, too."

I scooted over closer to him and rested my head on his shoulder. He put his arm around me and gave me a squeeze.

"Thank you," I said, and we both sat among the mess as he watched me attempt to dab the mascara stains from underneath my eyes and cheeks. After a bit, I began to put the items back in the box.

"I think you'd better help me put these things in the garage," I said, sealing the box. I knew letting go took discipline, and I also knew I couldn't keep these types of things in the cottage any longer.

*

The following week, on a late Saturday afternoon, John and I took the short bike ride over to Brewer Yacht Yard & Marina where he kept his 23-foot Formula powerboat in Oxford's harbor. Karen was comfortable enough to be left in charge for a couple of hours, and Colette packed us a little picnic dinner in a soft cooler bag that I stuffed into my bike basket, my camera flung around my neck. John had the drinks on his back in his manly backpack.

As we let go of the lines and John eased the boat out of his dock slip, I knew I was in for a treat. I hadn't been on a boat in years; my parents never owned one, so the only time I got out on one was if we rented a boat, or if I went out on a friend's boat when we lived in Annapolis, and that wasn't too often. John was an adept boater, and he guided us into the river without a problem. First up: we had to photograph the Inn from the water. Knowing that I wanted to take a ton of shots, John moved the boat around gently, helping to strategically position me so that I could shoot the Inn from different angles. He steered the boat as close as possible to the shore without running us aground, and I snapped away, happily trying different settings to see what effects might look best. We moved right and left, and I asked him to take me up and down Oxford's waterfront so I could incorporate other picturesque photographs into the website. He had incredible patience with my requests, as he moved the boat to and fro and here and there as I continued clicking the button on my camera.

Afterwards, we checked our voice mails on our cell phones and neither of us had a message from Karen. Just to make sure all was well, we called her, and she said everything was fine. It was her night to work late, and John and I decided to take advantage of the couple of hours we had to be out on the water before the sun would go down. John put the boat into high gear and we moved along the water, faster and faster, riding waves and wakes of other boats, feeling the rippling wind in our hair, and relishing the time we had away from the Inn. When he gave me the wheel for a bit, he taught me how to drive the boat, and I learned some boating rules. When we returned after it became dark, pulling the boat into its slip at the marina, we stayed on the boat and ate the remaining cheese and fruit Colette packed for us.

"This was nice," I said. "I can't wait to see how these photos look on the website. Do you want to see the shots on my camera?"

"No," he said. "I want to see what you do with them on the site. I can't wait to see the updated version. It really does need an overhaul."

"Okay," I said, "but don't hold your breath. It could be a while."

"You're in luck then," he said, "because I'm not going any-where."

CHAPTER 9

Weeks went by, the hot summer rolled in, and our small staff was into a routine. Darlene returned from Canada, after adding on another week to be with her family. Although she didn't work many hours—only about four a day—she took over cleaning the Inn's rooms and bathrooms, changing the linens, and attending to any other odds and ends that pertained to room upkeep. Her presence allowed me to focus more on the guests, the bookkeeping, breakfast and afternoon tea, and helping John with the grounds, in addition to the time I spent writing copy and taking photographs for the website. With Karen's help, we also decided to set up some social media accounts, including an Instagram feed and a Facebook page, and we even tackled Twitter. Things were coming together.

My sister kept her promise and told me she'd be down in a week to visit and to help with the website. When a guest cancelled the week prior, I blocked out that suite for her for the four days she would spend with us so she and Abbie could have their own privacy and not have to be crammed in with me. My fingers were crossed that Abbie was a better sleeper, especially for the sake of the other guests at the Inn. If not, I would swap with them and give Gracie my cottage, and I would stay in the Avon Suite.

In the midst of everything else that was going on, John took on the overwhelming task of dissecting the basement of the Inn, which still housed things from my grandparents. My mother asked him to clean "anything non-sentimental" out of the house, and stated that the project was long overdue. He was spending about two hours a day down there, and I would pop down on occasion to see if I could lend a hand, or if he needed me to help figure out if something was "non-sentimental." I knew he was nervous that he might toss something away that shouldn't be tossed. When we had questions, I would call my mother and father, and they'd let me know what they thought. A couple of circumstances required me to take a photo of the item and text it to my mother to see whether or not it was a "keeper."

I was sitting on the lawn in an Adirondack chair sipping my morning Hazelnut coffee after cleaning up breakfast, when John approached me with something in his hand.

"You've been in the basement for hours already today," I said, wanting him to know I knew he was down there working hard.

"Take a look at this," he said, handing over a large, leather-bound book with an embossed fleur-de-lis on the front.

"What is this?" I asked.

"It looks like a treasure," he said.

"Does it have gold in it?" I asked, teasingly.

"No, a different kind of treasure. Take a peek," he said.

I opened the book, and found it to be an old diary of some kind. The writing was in a very angled cursive, and the words had little spacing between them. The ink was faded, the paper yellowed, but the words were still legible, though somewhat challenging to decipher. I flipped through the pages, trying to figure out who the author was—and to see if the cursive was consistent throughout the book. Scattered among the pages were sketches and drawings, one, in fact, that resembled the Oxford Harbor and a large ship.

After a few minutes of reading some of the entries, with John sitting on the arm of the chair, leaning over, peering at the book, I said, "I think this is my grandmother's writing."

I skimmed down through it and found something intriguing. I struggled to dissect the cursive, and read the excerpt aloud to John:

22 October 1928

I am but eighteen, and last month, I married my husband, Ferio, who longs to captain a ship. Although we have little money, I know not what our future holds or how long a duration we will spend in this town, but it is his town from his upbringing, and he admires it so. At present, I have work as a seamstress and he is a waterman; I am beholden to so many generous folks who have helped us, yet I know not what lies ahead for us, either. He is a doting husband, an excellent and thorough thinker, and he is besotted with the sea. In fact, I chide him often and tease him saying that he may be more besotted with the sea than with his own wife! I don't begrudge this or find it troublesome in the least, for what is endearing and intriguing about my darling Ferio is his passion for life. At present, there is such happiness between us. I cannot imagine a better existence for Ferio and me. He always calls me "My Rosa."

I stopped reading there, and looked out across the river.

"Why did you stop reading?" John asked.

"The entry is dated 1928—right before the Great Depression."

"And?" he said, curiously.

"My grandfather's name wasn't Ferio; it was Edward," I said.

*

It was disconcerting to think that a thirty-seven year-old woman didn't know the history of her own family. Had this been kept from me? From my sister? Did my mother know? Did my own mother know that before her father, Edward, there was another man in her mother's life? And if so, why were we never told about Ferio?

The journal's pages were filled with writings, poetry, and sketches, all seemingly written by my own grandmother. I was determined to read all that she disclosed on the pages.

"Were there any other journals or books like this that you found?" I asked John later that afternoon after I spent an hour reading through some of the entries.

"That was the only one I found," John said.

"I want to see where you found it," I said. "I want to see what else is down there."

We made our way down the musty basement stairs to where John had piles sorted and organized. I walked around inspecting his progress. I hadn't gone into the basement in a couple of days, and it looked much more organized than it did the last time I visited; some piles were marked "keepers," and John had taken many loads of trash and unwanted items to the dump or to Goodwill in Easton.

"You didn't find anything else like it, right?" I asked.

"I promise you, Milly, had I found anything remotely like what I gave you, I would have shown it to you, just as I did with that one. I promise. There were no other personal things. Just a lot of junk and old clothes."

I knew he would have shown me anything else worthwhile, so I thanked him for all his work, and left it at that. But the discovery was so intriguing. I decided I would sort through Nana's journal before I discussed it with my mother. It was her mother's most intimate thoughts I was talking about, after all, and I wanted to be certain I had the story straight. I felt like part snoop and part investigative journalist.

I couldn't wait to get started.

*

That night, after a full day's work, John and I met in the kitchen for his weekly muffin making, only this time I brought the journal with me. As I sat there, reading, if I came across something interesting, I read an excerpt to him. I think he was happy for the conversation and the education about my family. I, too, was fascinated, and became wildly intrigued by the nature of hearing my grandmother Rosa's words.

"Listen to this," I said, and began to read aloud:

Ferio has been away for days as a waterman and fisherman, and I am left in the small house alone. The neighborly woman next door, Ethel, promises to look after me, as my own parents are more than two hours away, and are tending to my younger siblings. As the oldest, I married young to unburden them from the financial responsibilities of having to care for me, plus I found much love with Ferio. Finding work is becoming more challenging, and men are losing their jobs, some of them are even having to move to a new state for work and end up sending money home to their loved ones. Luckily for Ferio and me, people need food to eat, and the life of a fisherman who provides meals so far has allowed us to have a steady income, though we must endure long separations. As for me, I continue mending and making clothing, which helps us provide for each other.

"I've read so many stories about the depression, but it's different when you hear it from someone you knew who lived through it," I said.

"So what do you think happened between your grandmother and Ferio?"

"I don't know yet," I said. "But the journalist in me is dying to find out."

The timer went off, and John took a batch out of the oven. As he was tending to the muffins—taking one tray out and putting another tray in—I caught a glimpse of him in that apron, and it always made me chuckle.

"What's so funny?" he asked when he saw me smirking.

"You in that apron. I'm just so used to seeing you in your work and outdoor clothes—your 'handyman' and gardening clothes—that it makes me laugh when I see you so domesticated," I said.

"Laugh it up, Foster," he said, "I actually do have good taste in clothes. And you've not had the pleasure of seeing me looking sharp in a suit and tie."

"You're right. I never have seen you in a suit and tie."

"So that begs the question: would you like to see me in a suit and tie? Because I need a date for a friend's wedding the first weekend in August. Would you care to be my date?"

His casual, lighthearted approach caught me off guard. I put my hand between the pages of the book and closed it gently over my arm.

"Sure," I said.

I was looking at him.

I was looking at him differently.

CHAPTER 10

The cottage was dark except for the light beside my bed on the nightstand. I was under the covers with Nana's journal on my lap. There was something riveting about hearing her words come alive on the pages, and she was surprisingly a very good writer: descriptive, emotional, and informative. I had trouble picturing her as an eighteen-year-old bride, alone in the small house, Ferio working on the water, finding her way in small-town Oxford. I only remembered her as an older woman—grandmotherly—loving, sweet, and kind to all she met. These journal entries she wrote made me feel connected to her in a way I never was when she was alive, and I regretted immensely that she never personally relayed the stories that were here on these pages.

As I continued plodding along reading her thoughts on her life back in the early years of the journal, I gathered that as much as she adored, revered, and loved her husband, the lifestyle and times caused it to be a lonely time for her. She confessed to missing him tremendously when he was gone.

15 March 1930
Once again, I rattle around the small house at night, the fire blazing, the wind whipping through the windows, and it's cold—a very cold March.

Oxford is so quiet when the weather is fierce and keeps us indoors. I yearn for spring to arrive fully so that I may visit friends in Easton. Ferio is again on a ship on the Chesapeake Bay harvesting oysters, and I sit by the warmth of the fire writing this with very cold toes: oh, how I wish he were here keeping me warm and keeping me company!

That sense of loneliness was something I could relate to directly. I understood the pain of having no one around to talk to about matters of life or everyday living. I got the sense that Ferio could be gone a week or two at a time, but when he returned, Nana was filled with relief and satisfaction.

What was Ferio's last name? Which house was theirs and was it still standing? If it were, I wanted to go and photograph it. My curiosity got the better of me, and I found myself enthralled with Nana's journal, working through one journal entry at a time until I finally fell asleep at two o'clock in the morning.

*

"I see you two were at it again," Colette said when I dragged my tired body into the kitchen at seven-thirty promptly.

"The muffin man and I stayed up late, and then I stayed up even later reading what John found in the basement."

"What did John find in the basement?" Colette asked, completely unaware of our discovery.

"My Nana Rosa's leather journal filled with the writings of a happy but sometimes lonely woman during the depression."

"Wow," Colette said. "Riveting reading?"

"I'm making my way through it. My grandfather's name was Edward, but that is not the name of the man she married in 1928."

"Your grandmother was married prior to marrying your grandfather?"

"It appears that way," I said. "And the funny thing is, I didn't know this."

"But your mother knows, right?"

"I'm about to find out," I said.

I picked up the platter of French toast Colette made and brought it into the dining room. There were two older couples in the room having coffee and sitting at one of the tables together. I went back to the kitchen to set out the syrup and butter, when one of the women called out to me.

"Excuse me, I think we need some help here!"

Both Colette and I ran into the room and saw the woman's husband, who was bending over in his chair trying to catch his breath, complaining of chest pains. "Colette, call 9-1-1," I shouted.

I told him to breathe slowly and that an ambulance was on

the way. Hearing the commotion, John entered the room and sat next to the man. He remained calm, his voice steady. "Are you allergic to aspirin?" he asked.

His wife answered no, and Colette ran to the medicine cabinet in the kitchen and produced aspirin and a glass of water. The man took the aspirin, and John continued to coach him, trying to steady his breathing. There were perspiration beads on the man's forehead, and John asked Colette for a cool, damp cloth.

Minutes later, the paramedics arrived and quickly situated him in the ambulance, speeding off to University of Maryland Shore Medical Center in Easton. His friends and wife followed the ambulance, and we all sat back and looked at each other, full of worry and saddened by the event.

"I hope he's okay," I said, stunned by what occurred. "How did you know to give him an aspirin?" I asked John.

"My father had a mild heart attack a couple of years ago, and we asked the doctors what to do if it should ever happen again. It's one of the precautions you actually can administer before paramedics arrive, provided there is no allergy."

"Excellent thinking," I said, my head reeling from the excitement. "I hope he'll be okay."

We cleared their dishes away from the table, and John, Colette, and I worked in silence, all of us a bit shaken by the event. My cell phone rang, and I noticed I'd missed several calls from Karen, who was calling from the office.

"Is everything okay? What happened with the ambulance?" Karen asked, a worried tone in her voice.

"The ambulance took one of our guests, Mr. Keating, to the hospital. He was having chest pains and shortness of breath."

"Jeez," Karen said. "I hope he's okay."

"Me, too," I said.

*

My mother picked up the phone on the fourth ring, just as I was expecting to leave a message in her voice mailbox.

"How's my girl?" my mother asked as she picked up.

"Well, we've had an exciting morning," I said. "One of the guests at the Inn had symptoms of a heart attack, we think. He's at the hospital in Easton now."

"Oh dear," my mother said. "Is he going to be okay?"

"We're waiting for word from his wife," I said. "Scary stuff, and a lot of responsibility to get help. I told Colette to call 9-1-1 right away, and John gave him an aspirin as we waited for paramedics to arrive."

"Right—I remember John telling me that happened to his

dad a couple of years ago. Good thinking, John!" she said.

"John also found something interesting when he was cleaning up the basement: a journal that belonged to Nana from when she was 18 right before the depression." I waited to see how my mother would respond to that.

"I bet that's interesting reading," my mother said.

"It is," I said tentatively, "especially the part about Ferio."

"Who's Ferio?"

"Nana's first husband," I said, and I could swear I heard my mother's phone hit the ground.

*

I spent the next hour talking to my mother, reading excerpts to her of her own mother's writing, and the two of us wondering why she never told her own daughter of her first husband. Plus, I hadn't read far enough into the journal to know exactly what happened to Ferio. Divorce was not something a lot of folks did back in those days, and I didn't even want to imagine a worse fate for Ferio.

My poor mother was stunned by this revelation, and expressed a mixture of utter surprise and resentment that her mother never told her. "I will want to read it in its entirety when I get back," she said. "So, don't lose it. I just don't know what to say. I feel cheated."

"I know. I hesitated to even tell you."

"You had to tell me, Milly. That's my mother we're talking about! Why would she have kept it to herself all those years?"

"I'm not really sure, Mom. But her writing is really something. It's like you can hear her voice."

I promised her that I would keep her posted on my findings, and that I might do a little more digging to find out where they lived and what Ferio's last name was. There had to be a way to find old records, and then it dawned on me: Miles. Miles with his infinite wisdom, research skills, and a staff to help might be able to assist me with finding out more details and history.

*

"I need the number to Miles Channing," I said to Karen as I burst through the door of the office. "Find his recent reservation and the contact phone number he left us. I have to get in touch with him immediately."

John looked up, and I could see him staring at me as if I were a madwoman.

"Why do you need to call Miles?" he asked.

"He may be able to help me with some information I'm trying to get about Nana," I said, matter-of-factly.

Karen was rummaging through the reservation log book, and I logged onto the computer to see if I could track it down that way. I scrolled through our master guest list.

"I've got it!" she said triumphantly, beating me to it.

I wrote down his cell number on a scrap piece of paper, and began to walk outside the office and out onto the lawn. The birds were chirping and the heat index was unbearable, coupled with the humidity, but I needed to talk to Miles privately. Even though John knew about the contents of the journal, I wanted to ask Miles the favor without someone looking over my shoulder.

"Miles Channing," he said as he answered, not recognizing my cell phone number. Despite that we shared an enjoyable evening out, we did not exchange personal contact information.

"Miles, hi, it's Milly Foster from Inn Significant."

"Hey, how are you? And by the way, I would know who you are without mentioning the name of your business."

"Good, great. How are you?"

"Busy and completely overwhelmed since I last saw you, but fine. You?"

"I'm well, thanks. Actually, I have a huge favor to ask you and some of your top-notch researchers who help you gather information. Can you find the last name of a man named Ferio who lived in Oxford? His wife's name was Rosa. They married in 1928. She was born in 1911, and he was born around then, as well, though I don't know his exact date of birth."

"I can certainly see what I can find, and I'll ask some of the best hacks in the office to get on it. Who are Ferio and Rosa?"

"Rosa was my grandmother who was married to my grandfather, Edward. They are my mother's parents who owned the property that became the Inn. But a recent discovery has led me to uncover that Rosa was married prior to marrying my grandfather—to a man named Ferio."

"I see. Some interesting family history."

"Family history that was otherwise unknown," I said. "My mother nearly fell over when I told her that her mother was married before she married her father."

"Wow…good stuff," Miles said. "How did you find all this out?"

"John uncovered a journal in the basement of the Inn that belonged to Rosa. I'm still reading through it, but I'm desperate to find out any additional information I can."

"Didn't I tell you that you might want to reconsider writing?"

"I have to admit, Miles, I do feel a little bit like a journalist again."

"Welcome back," he said.

*

It turned out that our guest, Mr. Keating, suffered from a rather severe panic attack, and apparently those symptoms can sometimes be similar to those of a heart attack. News of his mother's illness reached him while he was on vacation, and the poor fellow was debating whether or not to hop on a plane and go back to California to be with her. The stress of the decision must have caused his anxiety, and I felt awful for him. John told me the news as I sat behind the desk in the office writing up facts about the Inn as I prepared for my sister's visit.

"What an absolute relief," I said, as I looked up from the work and leaned on the desk to look at John. "It's been weighing on my mind all day. I'm so sorry he was in such a state."

"They're on their way back here as we speak, and his wife said they will stay the night, but they're flying back to California tomorrow to be with his mother," he said. "It sounds as if she is gravely ill."

"So sad," I said.

"Do you have a minute? I want to show you something."

We left the office for a moment, putting the "Be Back in 10 minutes sign" on the door as Karen had already left for the day, and I followed John around to the side of the Inn where we had planted the garden. He bent down on one knee and reached out for one of the plants.

"Our first pepper, and over here, our first tomato. Things are coming to life in this little food garden."

I smiled. This was a project we tackled together, with a lot of coaching from Colette—a little slice of something new and different that we created at the Inn. I stopped to observe all the growth in the garden: the cucumbers, two pumpkins and their vines, the tomato and pepper plants, and some of our herbs were coming to life. I looked at him in amazement.

"Wow, look at that," I said. "It's going to be a really cool food garden. And it might make it onto the blog, if I actually get one going. I need to grab my camera."

He smiled back and appeared to be incredibly pleased with himself.

A few days later, my sister and Abbie arrived in her silver van. She slithered out of the driver's seat in a flattering, figure-slimming sundress, her blonde, highlighted hair bouncing with curls, sunglasses propped on the top of her head. John was kind enough to greet my sister and niece with me in the driveway and haul all their bags to their suite. A toddler, Abbie could get around and was the spitting image of my sister, her blonde hair thickening and curls surrounding her cherub face. Abbie immediately darted off toward the lawn, Gracie following her every step of the way. Gracie handed me a ball and encouraged me to kick it to Abbie. She loved chasing after it.

"The place looks amazing, Mill. I always forget just how stunning a piece of property this is. Look at that view of the water and the quietness of the setting. I hope guests appreciate just how special this place is," Gracie said.

"I think they do. I just spoke with a woman yesterday morning who comes every few months from D.C. and calls it her 'personal retreat.' She's one of Mom's regulars," I said.

We strolled the lawn, looking at the gardens, the hydrangeas popping out their colorful pink, blue, white, and purple blooms while the lavender covered some of the beds along the perimeter of the house. The lawn was meticulously manicured thanks to John's work on the John Deere. He spent hours mowing the grass each week and weeding the beds, and I wondered sometimes if he ever grew weary of all the maintenance, but he never complained. We walked over to the food garden, and her eyes grew wide.

"You planted this? You—the person who has been known to kill a cactus?"

"Well, I sort of directed it along with John and Colette. John did most of the planting, but I helped a little. It's pretty cool though, right?"

"I think you may have found yourself a little niche in this world, Mill. Gil would probably be so happy for you. I remember how much he loved this place."

"It's only temporary," I said. "But it's been great to be away from D.C. and see new scenery each day. I don't know what took me so long to move out of that house."

"You just needed to be ready."

She walked over to me and hugged my shoulders. "I know," she continued, "it's just great that you're here. I would imagine most of the guests are from nearby?" My sister was clearly moving away from discussing Gil again; she was not one to dwell on misery for too long. She was like my mother that way.

"Actually, I've got Karen, our college student and office assistant for the summer, creating a spreadsheet so we can do a better job of tracking just where our guests come from. I think it will help Mom and Dad with their marketing."

"And what about the website? Are we ready to start loading some things up?"

"I've written some better copy, I think. And I've taken a ton of pictures. Did you design a template?" I asked her.

"Yes, and I can't wait to show it to you—I think you're going to love it."

"And I have some news to tell you, too," I said, ready to unload all that I knew from Nana's journal thus far, having kept it to myself until I saw Gracie in person. I didn't want to mention it over the phone like I had done with my mother. "Did Nana ever mention a man named Ferio to you?"

"No, why?"

"Apparently, Nana was married to someone before she married Grandpa."

*

While Abbie napped in the stroller next to us in the shade, Gracie and I sat at the picnic table on the lawn sipping lemonades and eating cucumber sandwiches and freshly cut watermelon courtesy of Colette. We were hunched over Nana's journal. After relaying all that I knew thus far, I think she was just as fascinated as I was, and she combed through the pages, looked at the sketches, and read some of the excerpts. I wanted to read it cover to cover, and not jump ahead, but Gracie landed on an entry and read it aloud to me:

15 September 1931

Ferio came home earlier this evening exhausted from his excursion on the Bay. He sleeps little, and I am worried for his safety and health. He grows tired in the evenings when he is home, often falling fast asleep by eight o'clock. His face has become so tanned and lined from all of his hours in the hot sun on the water. As for me, my hands are tired from sewing all day long, pricking myself at least five times a mend, but times are hard, and food is not as plentiful as it once was, primarily because work moves at a very slow pace. Townsfolk are struggling, and they are working longer hours for less pay, as are we. At some point, these trying times will pass, I am certain, but for now, it feels like an endless wait for improvements. I pray regularly, hoping God will hear my request on behalf of all of us. I spent the day canning vegetables and fruits from the garden to store for the upcoming winter season. And still, I am without a child to love and call my own.

I suppose I should be thankful that I have this journal. It was a wedding gift from Ferio, and I promised him it would be a place where I express my thoughts. My father always believed in education, and there were many Saturdays that I would help him write and prepare his sermons. Sometimes we would spend hours revising what he was going to say to his parishioners. My mother, who is a schoolteacher, put books in my hands when I was very little. She taught me to read, and we would often read stories aloud to each other. I take great pleasure in reading, and have often thought I should have been a schoolteacher myself. I'm ever so thankful to both my parents for my ability to sit and write. It fills the time and helps the long days seem just a little bit shorter.

"She sounds so sad," Gracie said.

"The Great Depression hit everyone hard. I don't ever remember her talking about it, though. Do you?" I asked her.

"Not at all. And she's only been gone for ten years, so you would think she might have wanted to tell us just how difficult those times were for her."

"But she wasn't with Grandpa then, so maybe she just chose not to talk about it."

"Maybe he didn't want her to talk about it," Gracie said.

"Well, that's certainly a possibility," I admitted. Maybe that was the case. Maybe they decided together that her life with Ferio would not be discussed, would not be brought into this marriage, would not be a part of their life together. It was quite possible. In fact, back in Washington, D.C., I knew a woman who was divorced with teenagers and she never told them she had been married before she married their father. Her rationale was that the church annulled the marriage, so in their eyes and hers, it was as if it never really happened.

"What happened to Ferio?" Gracie asked, trying to move the pages along to the back of the journal.

"Oh, no you don't. I want to get there chronologically. Don't move ahead. I've got to stay with the story the whole way through."

"Don't you want to know now?"

"Of course I do. But I want to unearth all of this as a process, as Nana experienced it. It feels like it would be a disservice to her not to hear it told from beginning to end."

"So maybe that's why she wrote it down instead of verbally telling us. So that it would be documented in her own words..." Gracie said.

"...to unburden herself and let her story live on the pages," I concluded.

Just then, a white dove fluttered down and landed on the lawn, and she gazed at us, unafraid and emboldened, as she circled the table, stopped for a moment, and then took off into the afternoon sky, her body and wings graceful as she soared into the radiant sunshine and periwinkle sky.

*

My phone vibrated and Miles's number popped up.

"I've got to take this," I whispered to my sister as I grabbed the phone and walked away from the picnic table toward the water so I wouldn't wake Abbie. The sun was beating down on me, and I was without a hat or sunglasses, so I held one hand over my eyes, while the other one held the cellphone to my ear.

"Hi, Miles," I said.

"Greetings from New England," he said.

"On assignment?"

"Yes…writing a piece about how beautiful Portland, Maine is in the winter, even though it's the middle of summer."

"Well, I bet you don't have the smothering humidity we have here."

"You're right about that," he said. "But I do have some information for you."

"Okay, shoot."

"My sleuths have found out that Ferio's name was Ferio Di-Blanco. He was born in Italy, but his family immigrated to America, though we could only find the father's name to be Franco DiBlanco. We couldn't find any records regarding the mother's name, although we believe they all came together. She may have come through Ellis Island with a different surname, we're not quite sure. Nonetheless, Ferio married Rosa as you said in 1928, they had no children, and it looks as if Ferio and Rosa lived in a house on 21 Bank Street in Oxford."

"Twenty-one Bank Street. Wow. Good work. I don't have a pen in my hand because I'm out on the lawn—is there any chance you could text that information to me? I'd be so grateful."

"No sweat," he said. "Have you learned anything else from the journal?"

"Lots, but I'm not through reading it yet, and my sister just arrived with my niece from the Philly area, so she'll be here for a few days. Guess what she's helping me with? You'll be proud."

"Let me guess…the website?"

"Bingo," I said. I could hear a woman's voice in the background urging him to get off the phone.

"Well done. I can't wait to see the improved version. I've got to run, Milly, but I'll send all that over to you later today. Let me know if I need to put my aces on any other information gathering for you."

"I appreciate what you found out, Miles," I said, and he was off.

*

"You look nice. Where are you off to this evening?" I asked John, unaware of his social plans.

"Dinner with my parents. It's been a while."

"Nice," I said. "Have fun."

He bent down to see Abbie, and talked to her, asking her what her doll's name was. Abbie wasn't speaking too much yet, which worried my sister, but an occasional "Ma" and other small words would pass her lips. I told Gracie not to be concerned—that soon she would be talking nonstop. John was hoping to get her to say a few words, and I could tell she liked John because she smiled every time he was near her.

Gracie and I watched him go as he walked through the gate and out onto the street. Pope's on S. Morris Street wasn't far, and it was his parents' favorite restaurant.

"So, I hate to bring it up, but I have to ask you, and it's only because I care so much," she said. "Did you stop coloring your hair after Gil died?"

I didn't mind when she asked questions. She was a straight shooter, always had my best interest at heart, and knew wholeheartedly how Gil's death devastated me. I think that's why I didn't mind talking with her about it. She had spent many nights hearing me wail into the phone, and sometimes she just let me cry as she listened on the other end.

"Kind of."

"I'm making an appointment for you to go get that mess fixed. You need fresh color and a cut."

"It's that bad?" I asked.

"Worse. You need to take better care of yourself. How have the meltdowns been? Less rather than more, I hope."

"Getting better, minus one embarrassing catastrophe so far that poor John had to witness."

"What happened?"

"I opened a box of Gil's stuff when I was putting things away and had asked John to stop over and help me cart the stuff to storage. He found me in a heap on the floor, a crying mess."

"To be expected," Gracie said. "If I opened a box of Cal's stuff after he'd been gone and I was still in mourning, I would expect the same to happen."

"Thanks for making me feel like I'm not nuts," I said.

"You're not nuts. Gil was near perfection and you two suited each other. But that's not to say there isn't someone else out there for you, you know. And he just might work at this Inn."

I looked at her for a moment, and then back at the water. As sweet as John was, and as charming as he was, and as thoughtful as he was, I wasn't ready to pursue another relationship. With anyone.

It just wasn't in the cards right now. My heart was still so closed off and aching. How could I even think of letting go of Gil forever like that? Wouldn't I be doing our relationship a disservice? How would that be honoring his memory?

I didn't say any of this aloud to my sister. Abbie was getting hungry, and we needed to make ourselves something to eat for dinner. Plus, I hadn't yet cleaned up the porch from afternoon tea.

*

When all was settled and Abbie was tucked in for the night fast asleep in the Pack 'n Play we set up for her, my sister and I sat at the pine table in the kitchen with our laptops and got to work. The baby monitor was beside us so we could hear if Abbie stirred or cried, and I poured two glasses of wine for each of us.

"It's nice to have adult time," Gracie said, "even if we are working."

"We better not polish off a bottle or we'll make a mess of things," I teased.

We began by perusing the mass collection of photographs I took over the last couple of months, and decided which to keep and which to toss. We organized the pictures into folders so it would be easy to place them on the site: interior shots, exterior shots, garden, lawn and river, activities, Town of Oxford, St. Michaels, Easton, and Inn personnel.

"You must have spent hours taking these photos," she said. "I'm glad it's kept you busy."

"And here's all the copy I've written," I said, scrolling through my Word document.

Gracie opened up the template for the site she'd created, and it was perfect. She had miraculously combined all the aspects of websites Karen and I had sent her as examples into this perfect one for the Inn. She'd deleted the old account and created this new site that was not yet published, and wouldn't be until we were done building it. We had three days to finesse and polish it before Gracie had to leave. For the time being, if someone Googled our Inn, they would get a message that said, "Website under construction." That was the best we could do until it went live again.

We spent three hours putting things into place, and I marveled at how adept Gracie was with technology. I knew a little, but she knew a lot. She even knew how to link all of our social media to the site. It was coming together step by step. I liked the clean lines of the pages, the use of white space, and the way the text was going to be easy to read. There was something warm and welcoming about the design, and I felt it reflected the sense of the Inn beautifully.

Our goal for the evening was to get three sections formatted. When we finished working on it, John came through the door to check on us.

"How are you two making out with the site?" he asked genuinely.

"Come and see," I said, holding out the chair for him to sit next to me. "How was dinner with your parents?"

"Good," he said.

Gracie walked him through each aspect we'd built, and I could see he was impressed. And no wonder. It was stunning. He loved the look of it, too.

"It's not too feminine, is it?" I asked him.

"It's pretty," he said, "but not too feminine. It makes the Inn look incredibly appealing."

"It is incredibly appealing though, right?"

"It certainly is to me," he said, lifting his eyes to meet mine.

I felt my sister give me a little nudge under the table, and I almost felt the corners of my mouth turn upwards.

Almost.

CHAPTER 12

On the day my sister was set to return home, I ran back to the kitchen to fill Abbie's sippy cup with water for the ride back to Pennsylvania. We stayed up late the night before putting the finishing touches on the website, and InnSignificant.com launched shortly after midnight. I was so happy with the progress and the new look, I couldn't wait to tell my parents. My fingers were crossed that they would find it a pleasant and welcome surprise.

As I opened the door and stepped onto the front porch, I saw my sister deep in conversation with John as they stood next to the van. Not wanting to disturb them, I stayed back, out of sight, and watched them talk. I watched her body language and observed him listening intently to whatever it was she was saying. They were speaking in hushed tones, so I couldn't decipher any of it. She adjusted her little straw hat and sunglasses, and then began to buckle Abbie into the car. At that point, I walked down the stairs and over to them.

"Here's the water for Abbie," I said.

"Thanks so much, Milly. I had a great time. I hope Mom and Dad will be happy with our little collaboration."

"I honestly don't see why they wouldn't be—it looks phenomenal."

"I agree. It really looks fantastic," John said. "You two might have a career in website facelifts."

"One never knows, I suppose," I said.

I hugged my sister and kissed her on the side of her head, setting her hat askew.

"Drive safely, and call me when you get in. Give my love to Cal," I said as we embraced.

And then she whispered in my ear and patted me on the back. "You seem like you again," she said. "And don't forget your salon appointment."

John and I stood next to each other waving goodbye as the van made its way through the gate and onto the road. It was early, and breakfast at the Inn was being served.

"After we clear up the dining room, want to go for a quick bike ride for some ice cream? It's so stinking hot, and I'm dying for something sweet. I think Karen can hold down the fort for a bit, especially if we promise to bring some back for her," John said.

"Sure, if she's okay for a while. I'll grab the cooler bag for her pint. But I have to be back before one. I have a two o'clock appointment off-site."

"Anything you want to tell me about?" he asked.

"Not really," I said, smiling.

*

We lathered up with sunscreen, our hats, and sunglasses, and began the short trek to the Creamery. July weather could be brutal, and today was one of those days. The lack of a breeze made it that much hotter, but we pedaled on, with cones of ice cream as our goals. I knew he could afford to eat those calories, as I saw him running earlier in the morning before my sister left, but as for me, I'd been sitting on my butt for the last few days up to my neck in website work. It was good to be riding the bike.

We each got a cone—he ordered the Fresh Cut Strawberry, while I picked the Double Belgian Chocolate—and we found a spot in the shade near the water.

"So, you're still okay to attend that wedding, right?"

"Yes," I said. "Two weeks from now, right?"

"You got it. It's a six o'clock wedding on August 4 in St. Michaels, so I've asked Karen to work that evening so we can go. Colette will be on call, and may even hang out at the Inn with her husband that night just in case Karen feels uncomfortable."

"That's awfully nice of them," I said. "I'm actually planning on getting a dress today when I run my errand."

Two kids ran by us, chasing each other to the water with enormous squirt guns that were almost bigger than they were. I secretly wished they would spray me with them. I could hear the mothers calling after them not to soak anyone nearby.

"Do you remember what it was like to be a kid?" he asked.

"Do I!" I said. "What a great time of my life. Absolutely no responsibility."

"It's a shame childhood doesn't last longer. I have such great memories of playing Hide & Seek, SPUD, chasing fireflies and putting them in jars, running through the sprinkler, playing Little League ball, taking our inflatable canoes into the river, and riding our decorated bikes in the annual Fourth of July parade. Now all kids seem to want to do is play video games or stick their noses in iPhones."

"You are right about that. My childhood was spent away from the television in the summer. I was constantly outside. I remember building a tent made out of old sheets and blankets and begging my mother to let me sleep in it outdoors. Gracie and I would string twinkle lights inside it and believed fairies were in the trees in the back. We got spooked in the middle of the night and ran inside with our sleeping bags. We ended up sleeping in the sleeping bags on the screened-in porch instead with all the lights on."

We were both trying to eat our ice cream quickly because the ninety-eight degree temperature was making them melt rapidly. When we finished, John had a little bit of strawberry on his nose.

"You've got a spot right there," I said, pointing to where the ice cream sat on his face.

"Saving it for later," he joked, as he wiped it away with a napkin.

*

When I returned at five from taking care of my two errands in Easton, I got out of the car with a dress wrapped in black plastic still on the hanger. John was on the porch tending to the afternoon tea and saw me get out of the car as he was cleaning up, plates in hand. He walked down the steps.

"Need a hand with anything?" he called from across the lawn.

"Nope. I've got it," I said. He looked as if he'd showered after ice cream and before tea. He was all neat and tidy and walked a little closer. I got a whiff of his cologne.

"Look at your hair," he said. "You look like a million bucks."

"My sister encouraged me to freshen up and get some highlights, only I don't believe she said it quite that way. I believe her words were something along the lines of 'do something with that mess.' I guess it's a good thing I listened to her."

"Well, you look great. And is that your dress for the wedding?"

"Yes, but like the bride, you don't get to see it until the wedding day."

"Fair enough," he said. "What are you doing for dinner?"

"Not sure, but I'm starving. I haven't eaten since the melted ice cream."

"Well, I think Colette may have been up to her old tricks. I think she left something for us tonight."

"Really? I'm intrigued," I said.

I excused myself to put my new dress in the cottage and take a quick shower. I didn't want to wash my hair because the stylist did such a nice job on it, blowing it dry first then using a flat iron. My dark hair got some lighter, caramel streaks in it, and she even gave me a few bangs in the front with layers for volume. I absolutely hate to say my sister was right, but she was. After I toweled off, I slipped into one of the dresses I bought from Dragonfly and applied some makeup. I stared at myself in the mirror and almost didn't recognize the person staring back at me. She looked healthier, with a suntan and rosy cheeks, and her hair, just past her shoulders, was shiny with volume and good color. If only her mother could see her now; she would be so happy to see the change.

And then I got a crazy idea.

I grabbed my iPhone and stepped out onto the porch. I hit the camera button and switched the setting. I smiled big, and took a freaking selfie.

My first ever.

My contact list wasn't terribly long, but I found the text thread that included Mom, Gracie, and me. I attached the photo and wrote: "You and Gracie made me do this—new hair and a suntan. Thank you. XO."

And then I hit "send."

*

"Okay, what exactly did Colette have up her sleeve?" I asked John as I walked through the door to the kitchen. He was standing with his back to me, and I could tell he was fiddling with something.

"Looks like she made us some fresh steak salads, and if I'm not mistaken, I believe some of our own, homegrown produce might be included."

I rounded the corner of the kitchen cabinet and took a peek at Colette's handiwork. She was an amazing cook, chef, baker, and now, home-grown-salad-maker. The two salads were picture-perfect; they reminded me of a cover of a food magazine.

"She made this homemade sourdough bread on the side with a fresh pasta salad as well. And here is some cut up watermelon," John said.

"Looks like the perfect summer evening meal," I said. "Let's sit outside in the shade. There's a little breeze now, and it feels much better than it did this afternoon."

We carted everything outside to the open picnic table, the one where Gracie and I would sit and watch the boats go by. The weeping willow was softly blowing, and the lavender was rustling a little, allowing us to smell its fresh scent. At that very moment, I couldn't have asked for a better sky, lawn, garden, river, or company.

"Any other news from your grandmother's journal that you haven't filled me in on?" John asked as we sat and talked over dinner. It was the first time we fully took a moment to just sit and enjoy each other's company on site. Twice in one day, I thought. First, ice cream. Now this.

"I'm up to 1931, and Ferio is working on a boat that harvests oysters on the Chesapeake Bay. He's gone a lot, and Nana writes about being lonely and working hard. She also talks a bit about how difficult times were during the depression, and that they were barely getting by. Oh, and apparently, they must have been wanting a child, but they had no luck."

"It must be interesting to read her own words," John said. "I get most of my family history from my father, who loves to talk and will talk you to death."

"I need to meet them," I said.

"Would you like to?"

"Of course. Seems only fair seeing as how you know more

about my parents than you would ever need or want to know. It's only right that I have the same opportunity."

"Are you a glutton for punishment?" he teased.

"I very well may be," I said. "Although I'm sure your parents are lovely people. And what about your grandmother? When do I get the pleasure of meeting her?"

"She would love to meet you. I just saw her the other afternoon when you were with Gracie. She actually asked me, 'When do I get to meet the Inn-girl?'"

"She called me the 'Inn-girl?'"

"She did."

I laughed at that. Something about it was so funny. I mean, it actually was kind of hilarious. Three years ago I was one of the best writers at *Washingtonian Magazine*, and now I was serving tea, cleaning up, changing bed linens, helping plan itineraries, and making dinner reservations for people. But the crazy part was, I didn't mind it at all. In fact, it gave me a sense of purpose I never felt before with regard to work. And it wasn't hard work; it was just a lot of busy work. I catered to people all day long, but with an Inn that only has six rooms, it wasn't too terribly taxing. Plus, I had great people working with me—Darlene, Karen, Colette, and John were all tremendous—and we all seemed to genuinely like each other.

A younger couple, Stacy and David Anderson, who were

guests at the Inn approached John and me as we were sitting at the picnic table picking at the watermelon. She was pretty in a long maxi dress, her long blonde hair cascading down her back, and he looked sharp in his khaki shorts and Vineyard Vines t-shirt.

"Hi," David said.

"Hi, you two," I said. "Enjoying this warm summer evening?"

"We are," he said. "Rumor has it you might have a Bocce set."

"We do," John said.

"We do?" I said back.

"It belonged to Milly's grandfather. I started cleaning them yesterday, polishing them up and getting them ready for some action. But I think they may just be good enough to use. Let me go get those Bocce balls."

I was stunned. He had found them, but he hadn't told me. By the sound of things, it may have been a recent discovery from the basement. I couldn't wait to see them and touch them. Playing on the lawn with Grandpa was one of my favorite things to do when I would visit as a teenager. Sometimes, the whole family would have a little tournament, but Grandpa and I loved it the most.

"Your Inn is lovely," Stacy said. "We're having such a nice, relaxing time just being here alone. We have an 18-month-old at home, and she's with my mom so we can get two nights away for our anniversary."

"It's nice you can do that," I said. "And I'm glad you stayed here. It's my parents place—they own it."

"Yes, I know," she said. "I was reading about your parents, grandparents, and the history of the Inn on our drive over from Frederick this morning on your website."

"That is so good to hear!" I said.

A few minutes later, John emerged from the garage with the Bocce balls in a light blue box that I immediately recognized. They were Grandpa's. They looked exactly the same—the red balls and the green balls with the little white pallino.

"Bocce would be more fun with four playing, don't you think John?" David said.

"Girls versus boys?" I asked.

*

After the boys broke the game's tie, 2-1, we called it quits. The sun was almost all the way down, and we were having trouble seeing the ball in the grass. We wished the Andersons goodnight and walked the Bocce balls back to the garage.

"I'm so glad you found the Bocce balls. That was a lot of fun," I said. "Thank you."

"Thank you for having dinner with me and for playing."

"Any time," I said.

I started to walk over to gather the dishes and mess that we left at the picnic table, when John caught me yawning.

"I've got this. I'm sure you are tired from your late night with Gracie. Go relax," he said.

"Really? No, I should help you..."

"Not tonight. Tonight you get a 'get out of jail' card. Go. I've got this. Honestly."

"Are you sure?" I asked again.

He gave me a stare, and I knew what it meant.

"Okay. I will see you in the morning then?"

"See you in the morning," he said.

I walked back to my cottage completely contented with the last several days. Gracie and Abbie brightened my week, the website was functional (and people were reading it), and I took care of myself a little bit. I also won't deny that spending time with John had been fun. For a few moments I forgot what it was like to miss someone—to miss someone so much it physically hurt and left you incapacitated.

Chapter 13

At two-thirty in the morning, I shot straight up in bed. I heard rustling outside the cottage, and it frightened me. There were footsteps along the gravel pavement and what sounded like a groan. I wasn't sure if it was part of my dream or if it was real, but I tip-toed out of bed without turning on the light and peeked outside my front window.

There was a figure pacing back and forth.

John.

I gently opened the door, so I wouldn't startle him.

"John?" I called.

He stopped. He looked at me. Our porch lights allowed me to see that his face was red and streaked with tears.

"John?" I said again as I walked over to him.

"Don't," he said, as I approached. "Don't."

"What's going on? What's the matter?"

He continued walking back and forth, his head down as he looked at the ground. He was trying to catch his breath, and I was having trouble getting him to settle, to calm down. I made him stop and grabbed both of his hands; I looked him in the eyes.

"I'm here," I said. "You're okay. Breathe. Breathe in...exhale...slow it down a bit," I said softly, coaching him. This simple trick that Angela taught me after Gil's death helped me a great deal.

Not only had I been depressed, but anxiety got the better of me as well. I'd wake up in the middle of the night sweating and struggling to catch my breath. I knew what it was, and with her guidance (and a few drugs in the beginning), I was able to calm myself down. The technique had also worked for Mr. Keating, so I hoped it would work for John.

He breathed in. I asked him to sit next to me. We planted ourselves on the steps of his cottage. It took several minutes for his breathing to become more regular, and after about six or seven minutes, I sensed he was calming down and he began to come back.

"How often does this happen?" I asked him gently, not wanting him to feel defensive or embarrassed by what just occurred.

"Two or three times a year now. It's been much better since I've been here, but it still happens."

"I understand," I said.

"I'm sorry," he said. "I'm sorry."

"For what?" I asked him gently, not wanting to upset him any further.

"I didn't tell you the full story. I left some parts out."

"That's okay," I said. "We all edit our own stories."

We continued to sit as he got himself together, slowly, methodically, breathing in and breathing out. I held his hand. I remembered my mother doing the same for me in the aftermath of Gil's death. Just having her hand in mine helped. I rubbed the top of his hand as he concentrated on calming himself down.

"When I was deployed, there was an accident. Three men died. I was in the transport plane with my co-pilot. We just landed in Iraq, and were ready to unload supplies. The military vehicle was approaching with the three Army sergeants aboard. In minutes, they were gone, their bodies dismembered and a host of military personnel was trying to help. IEDs were planted in the ground, and they were everywhere, and it made us all cautious because you can't see them. But these soldiers had no chance, and after the explosion, there was nothing any of us could do. It was a massive one. Hundreds of pounds of explosives. The vehicle happened to hit the IED at just the right spot, and they were dead in an instant, all because they were coming to help unload supplies. I'd never witnessed anything like that before. That was my first. And then there was another time. One man went down after hitting an IED. The medic saved him, but he lost both his legs. I still have flashbacks, bad dreams, and night sweats. When I left the military, I thought I wanted to be a pilot for Delta, but I couldn't. I was jittery and too affected by it all, so I worked on the ground. After six years of that, I ended up here. There you go. That's the full story. I'm damaged goods, Milly."

"You're not damaged goods. And if you are, so am I. We're both suffering from the past, John. We're both trying to overcome traumatic experiences. And whatever these flashbacks are called, they make us relive the pain of having lived. The point is, we are alive while others may not be so lucky. And perhaps that is part of the problem—the guilt that we deal with. I'm constantly asking myself how I lived while others, like Gil, did not? You said yourself that life is hard sometimes. Maybe it just takes us longer to cope. Maybe our hearts are just more sensitive than others. At least that's what I try to tell myself. It has nothing to do with being damaged goods."

The half moon was high above the river, casting its glow along the calmness of the water. The shrill chirping of crickets prevented complete silence, and yet John was listening to me. We remained side by side, my hand in his, as we just sat, attempting to mirror the calmness and peacefulness that stretched out before us.

And perhaps that's why both of us were happy to be working where we were and not in Washington, D.C., alone in a house or working on planes in the military. Perhaps that's why time spent here, the chance to enjoy life, nature, the company of others, and to help make people happy in the simplest of ways, was exactly what suited each of us.

It was then that I wondered whether my mother and father must have known the healing powers of this place, and that maybe, just maybe, they believed that John and I had the power to heal each other. Maybe my mother's plan was even more hopeful and concocted than what she decided to tell me. Did my parents really have to go to Ireland? I believed in fate, but I also believed that sometimes a loving and caring mother knew how to maneuver fate in just the right manner so that the process of healing was pushed along ever so gently.

*

"Come inside and stay with me tonight," I said. "I promise, no funny business. Just you and me attempting to get some sleep or we'll both be worthless tomorrow."

He smiled a tender smile. He seemed to be coming back to the John I had gotten to know over the past couple of months.

"I don't want you to feel sorry for me," he said. "I couldn't stand it if you looked at me with pity."

"Okay, well, then, you can feel sorry for me and pity me then, because I won't sleep a wink unless I know you're doing better."

"If you have an extra blanket and a pillow, I'll sleep on your couch," he said.

I grabbed the extra blanket from the armoire and a pillow from my bed and brought it to him. I suggested that we turn on the television, and he agreed to that, probably not wanting to talk about anything further. I turned off the lights so that only the flicker of the television allowed us to see. I landed on Nick at Nite, the volume almost at a whisper, and tucked him in on the couch. John rested on his side, his head on the pillow.

"No need to wake me for my morning run," he joked.

I snuggled in a bit on the other end of the couch and pulled a blanket over my body. I leaned my head against the pillow and could feel my eyelids growing heavy. We'd spent so much time together over the last twenty-four hours that it didn't feel strange or awkward, but rather just as it should be right now. It was what I would do for any friend, and within the half hour, I fell asleep on the couch with him.

*

I won't lie about it. It was a little awkward in the morning when we realized we had slept together, platonically, of course, but still, sometimes there's a certain intimacy that comes from just such an act. I wasn't worried about not having my bra on last night when John was struggling with the past because I was too focused on him, but in the morning, it was a different story.

I ducked into my bedroom and grabbed a robe to throw over my thin tank top and he was stirring on the couch.

"Thanks for letting me sleep here," he said. "It actually was quite nice."

"I'm glad you're feeling better."

"I guess it's time to make the donuts, right? Colette is probably wondering where we are."

"I just want to make sure you're okay," I said, walking closer to him.

"I'm fine. Just you helping me through it made it less painful. And thanks for listening. I didn't mean to keep things from you."

"You didn't keep anything from me; you just weren't ready to share the story with me yet. No one knows better about keeping things to herself than I do."

He stood from the couch in his comfortable shorts and plain t-shirt, and began to fold the blanket. I asked him if he wanted coffee, and he said he wanted a shower first. I said I wanted to do the same, and as we walked to my door, he stooped down a little to meet my height and gave me a hug.

"Thanks again, Milly," he said.

CHAPTER 14

After breakfast was served and cleaned up and I profusely
thanked Colette for the dinner she prepared the night before for
John and me, I began my walk over to 21 Bank Street to photograph
the house where Nana and Ferio lived according to Miles and his research team. Gracie and I should have taken that walk together, but
time got away from us as we tried our best to manage a two-year-old,
the Inn, and rebuilding a website. I promised her I would email her
the photographs of the exterior.

I left John working outside in the yard riding the lawnmower
and keeping the grass meticulously manicured; something told me
he just wanted to be outside today in the fresh air and not have to
talk about his nightmare last night. The humidity had subsided a bit,
and the sun kept peeking in and out from behind the fluffy white
clouds that dusted the sky. I walked out Strand Street and could
see the Ferry just pulling into Oxford Harbor. I made the right at
the Robert Morris Inn on S. Morris Street, and continued to a left
on Tilghman Street until it met Bank Street. The homes in Oxford were charming, each unique and full of character, and I enjoyed
looking at one after the other, some with front porches, some with
dormer windows, and some with awnings. I always imagined living
in a quaint house like any of the ones I passed, and some reminded
me of my former home. Whether the home had a white picket fence

or not, I especially adored the flower boxes and gardens boasting colorful blooms reminiscent of old English gardens. There was no doubt that the summer months showcased Oxford at its finest.

There was a woman pulling weeds along the front, brick walkway outside 21 Bank Street, and I didn't want to seem rude as I stood in front of her house and snapped photographs. She didn't look familiar to me, although certainly my mother or father might know her. I hesitated, wondering if I should walk away or simply ask her if I might take pictures of her home. Not one for being timid—years of journalistic training taught me there's no time to be shy—I chose to speak to her, and just as I took a few steps toward her, she turned around.

"Beautiful morning, isn't it?" she said to me, garden gloves on her hands, a straw visor covering her face and protecting her from the sun. Her reddish hair was damp at the back of her neck, and her face was moist with perspiration. She was kneeling on one of those foam gardening pads. I made a mental note that we might need to purchase a few of those for the Inn to protect our knees.

"Yes," I said. "Stunning. I assume this is your home?"

"Oh, yes. We've been here forever, Richard and I, but I'm the one who tends to the garden. Do you live in Oxford?"

"I do," I said. "For the time being. My parents own Inn Significant, and I'm here for the year helping them out."

"Oh, lovely place, that Inn. How lucky for you to be able to stay there on the water! That would be my one request: to move this house to a plot of land right on the river. Must be glorious."

"It is wonderful, I won't deny that. My name's Milly, and I recently came across an old diary that belonged to my grandmother, and it appears that she and her first husband lived in your home back in 1928."

"Is that so?" the woman said. She stood and examined me inquisitively, wiped the dirt off her knees, and removed her gloves. She walked closer toward me.

"I'm Eva Bramble, and I have something that just might interest you."

*

I stepped inside the small Cape Cod, expecting it to be dated and filled with antiques, but what I found was exactly the opposite. Eva kept an incredibly tidy house that looked recently renovated. The wide-plank, maple floors were stunning throughout, and it looked as if walls had been removed to give the place a more open and airy feel. There was shiplap on the walls painted white, which added a touch of nostalgia and personality to the place. The furniture was on the newer side, the draperies were white with colorful pastel piping, and she had fresh flowers on all her tables. I could see that she took great pride in her home.

She asked me if I wanted to have a seat in her dining area after getting me a glass of cold lemonade. Richard was on the golf course for the day, so he was not at home. She returned a few moments later with an old shoebox in her hands.

"I'm wondering if this might belong to your family," she said.

I gently took the box from her hands; it was from Montgomery Ward & Co. with a drawing of a woman's Oxford—a black and white saddle shoe—on it. Though the box was faded, the label was still legible. I opened the lid, and swallowed hard. There were Ferry vouchers and a couple of envelopes; there were vintage coins and several dried, pressed flowers. At the bottom of the box was a pair of old, white gloves and a somewhat tangled, silver cross on a chain along with black Rosary beads and a church missal. There were two weathered photographs of my grandmother with a man I assumed was Ferio. They both looked so young, but there was no denying it was Nana in the photo. Positioned in front of a garden with a rose trellis, Nana wore a straight skirt with a pleated bottom, a sweater with a long scarf, socks, Oxfords, and a cloche hat. Her severely bobbed haircut that hit a couple of inches below her chin made her look incredibly chic, reminiscent of a Chanel model. Ferio was dapper in a solid blazer, shirt and tie, striped trousers, and two-tone wingtips. Both of them were young and slim and smiling. The picture was frayed at the edges, and the white frame that surrounded the image was worn and tattered.

"Is that your grandmother?" Eva asked.

"Yes," I said. "That is my Nana—Rosa. She must have been somewhere between eighteen and twenty-five here."

"She's lovely," she said.

"She was. And she lived here, in your house, with this man, Ferio," I said, pointing to Ferio in the photograph, his hair dark and wavy and eyes as dark as coal. "I cannot tell you just how special this is. Thank you."

"We found it several years ago, before we renovated. Actually, I can't take any credit for it at all, dear, except that the box was in the house. It was my contractor, Bob, who actually found it when he had to go into the crawl space to make some repairs. Richard and I had never been in there. I knew this box had to belong to prior own-ers, but I had no idea which ones. It seems there were two owners between the time your grandmother owned the house and when we purchased it. There are no names anywhere on any of the items, so I had no idea to whom they belonged. For some reason, I considered it a good omen—as if there was love in this house sometime before Richard and I moved in."

I smiled at the sweet, kindly woman, and reached into the

box. "I want you to keep this," I said, handing her the Rosary. Nana had given me one when I made my confirmation when I was fourteen, and that one was special to me.

"Oh, I couldn't—" she started to say.

"I insist. I want this to stay with you and the house. I don't believe it would be right to take it since there appears to have been many blessings in this place."

We sat at her kitchen table for at least a half an hour talking about Oxford, her time in the town, and how many friends she and Richard have made over the years. She told me how involved she is with the Garden Club and her husband is an avid golfer and yachtsman. Eva personally invited me to attend the next Oxford Ladies Breakfast in town. I happily accepted, thinking that if even half the ladies were as congenial and welcoming as Eva, I was in for a real treat. In return, I invited her to come and have afternoon tea at Inn Significant.

Without hesitation, she accepted.

*

With my camera slung over my shoulder and a shoebox in my hand, I walked back toward the Inn. I peeked into the office to see how Karen was doing, and I bumped into Darlene who was carrying sheets and towels to the laundry. John was pruning some of the trees along the property's fence.

"I've been trying to get into the King Suite to change the linens, but there must be some hanky-panky going on in there because that young couple has yet to emerge! They've got to come out at some point for air, don't they?" she teased.

I giggled. "One would think so," I said, barely able to get the words out.

Darlene had a great sense of humor, and was not afraid to be blunt. She could always make me laugh, and I often thought she missed her calling as a shock radio deejay. That comment coming from her was mild this morning.

Colette was still in the kitchen making cookies and bite-sized sandwiches for the four o'clock tea, and I wanted to help with that.

"Why don't you let me do this today so you can go home and spend some time with your husband?" I said to her as she began slicing a cucumber.

"But this is my job..."

"Not today," I said. "Today, you get to do whatever you want. Let me do it. John's got the lawn under control, Karen has things running as tight as a drum in the office, and Darlene's taking care of the rooms, provided the couple in the King's Suite takes a break from making whoopie, according to Darlene. I honestly don't mind.

My checklist of things to accomplish is small, so it's really no big deal."

Colette took a few minutes to show me where everything was, and she handed over her apron. "Are you sure?" she asked one more time, as I tried desperately to hide that I had become a little tired from the previous night's activities.

"Yes. It's beautiful outside. Take that beach chair of yours and a good book and go sit by the water with your cute husband."

"You think he's cute?" she asked, a devilish grin moving across her face.

"Adorable. Now get out of here," I said, teasingly.

She washed her hands and dried them with a towel. "What's in the box?"

"Do you know a woman named Eva who lives on Bank Street?"

"Eva Bramble? We have lunch once a month with the Oxford Ladies Group."

"Well, apparently, my grandmother lived in the house that is now Eva's. She found this box in the crawl space."

"Well, I'll be—" she said. "May I?"

"Of course."

She opened the lid and perused the items, fascinated by each one of them. She looked carefully at the pictures of Rosa and Ferio, and then gingerly held the gloves that I imagined must have belonged to my grandmother.

"I can see your mother in her," she said, studying the picture closely.

"I know."

"And not so surprisingly, I see aspects of her in you, as well."

*

John and I didn't spend any time together in the afternoon; he kept busy with his things and then went to visit his parents and his Uncle Paul, who was in town visiting with them. I was left to handle the Inn that night, and I didn't mind the solitude at all. When afternoon tea was over and all was back in order, I forwarded the main line to my cell phone, grabbed Nana's journal, and found a lone Adirondack chair. After seeing Nana's pictures today, I was more intrigued than ever to make my way though her journal—to find out what happened.

9 July 1932

I'm becoming more worried by the day. Work has almost come to a halt and Ferio is gone more than ever on the ship. The days seem long in the summer as the sun is out for hours, beating its heat down upon us, and the house is unbearably hot. I have one fan that circulates, but that's it. I try to find a spot outside in the shade to sit and do my work. My friend, Simone, is my saving grace. Her husband also works on the ships, and we bide our time talking, sewing, mending, strolling, and tending to the gardens. Sometimes, we even walk to the harbor and wade in the water in an attempt to stay cool. I long to read a good book, but I have already read everything we own, including Wuthering Heights and Rebecca three times each. Simone and I are thinking of exchanging the books we have, and we are trying to get others interested in doing the same. Since there is no library here, it would be a good way to share our books with each other. She and I have already exhausted what we have in our small collections.

25 July 1932

I accidentally cut my hand with a knife today when I was slicing the bread I made. Typically, when I make something, I make a lot of it and store it in the icebox. It took me a while to stop the bleeding. Even so, I was still concerned, and I had my nurse friend, Adelaide, take a look at it to make sure I didn't need any further treatment. She bandaged it up for me. I still have not heard from Ferio. He was supposed to be home today, but it's late and he has not yet arrived.

26 July 1932

Ferio returned late last night, exhausted. I fear he is not getting proper

sleep, for it is now one o'clock in the afternoon, and he has not yet awak-
ened.

I read through several other installments of her writing. Some of it was lovely while other parts were melancholy, including the loneliness that stretched out for days and seemed interminable; the fear of not having food to eat on the table; the worry for her husband's work that took him out on the tumultuous water through the storms and bad weather; and the need to rely so much on the kindness of others because her own, immediate family was not nearby. I took all of this into consideration as I read Nana's words over and over. She did not feel sorry for herself; she was just documenting each day as it played out. It was as if she simply accepted life for what it was and tried her best to tackle each day as it came. Her efforts to survive reminded me of what John said to me that day I cried over Gil's belongings: Sometimes we just have to accept that life is hard and it can be debilitating, but only if we let it be that way.

24 September 1932
I wore my old skirt and lightweight sweater with my scarf today to go to the market. Annalise Hopkins was there in a tailored dress, fabulous cranberry beret, and shiny new Mary Janes. I felt ragged and tired next to her. Her father is the mayor of Easton, and I suppose part of the job of the mayor and his family is to keep us all in good spirits through these dif-

ficult times. I found myself laughing to myself, thinking that just because it's the depression doesn't mean we don't like to look pleasing and fashionable. We still want to respectably present ourselves to our husbands, family, and friends. I want to do my hair and put on a little lipstick. I love red lipstick, but I have to use it sparingly. My tube is running low, and lipstick isn't something we can spend money on right now.

I considered myself luckier than Nana in one particular way—I didn't have to worry about money. My sole responsibility was to keep the Inn running as well as it did under the direction of my parents. While that was a big responsibility, I somehow believed that I wouldn't fail. I looked out across the water as a kayaker paddled by. The serene setting as the sun lowered in the sky was my favorite time of day. I loved early evening; it reminded me that the day was well spent and that the evening was yet to come. It wasn't that I had big plans or anything notable to do, but I'd enjoyed my languid moments at the Inn. Something told me my parents might have known I would, too.

As I stretched my legs and closed the journal for a bit, I wondered what Gil would think of my decision to do this—to come here and help my parents. Would he have thought it was wise of me to sell the house, pay no rent, and live on my parents' property for a year? I found myself feeling as if I were mooching off of them, because, in essence, that's exactly what I was doing. No rent. Low food costs. My car was already paid off. And I had received quite a hefty amount of money from Gil's life insurance plan and accidental death insurance. I had a lot of money just sitting in a bank and in investments.

My phone rang, and it startled me. My mother.

"Hello, love, how's it going?"

"Good. Guess where I'm sitting right now?"

"In the office paying bills."

"No, did that yesterday morning."

"In the kitchen eating some of Colette's yummy leftovers?"

"Nope," I said.

"I give up," she said.

"Sitting on the lawn in a chair reading Nana's journal. It's so beautiful here this time of day."

"It's my favorite," she said. "Anything new?"

I told her about Eva and the box, about the photographs of her mother and Ferio, and about the journal filled with Nana's thoughts. She listened intently, and I promised to take a picture of the photo and text it to her when we hung up so she could see it. I guess I expected her to be more surprised by the coincidence of Eva Bramble's box, but I guess nothing could top the fact that she didn't know her own mother had been married before.

"Mom—can I ask you something?"

"Anything, you know that."

"Did you really have to go to Ireland, or was it something you concocted to help steer me off the path of self-destruction and misery I had created for myself?"

"Sweetie, I love you, but you know me better than that. You know I'll confess to nothing," she said.

CHAPTER 15

The afternoon of August 4th arrived, and I knew in a couple of hours I would be on the way to a wedding: the marriage of Greg and Mona, two of John's oldest friends, both divorced, a second wedding for both of them. One hundred guests were expected to attend, and I presumed John would know a lot of people since he grew up and went to school with the bride and groom. They both had married people they met in college, and when those first marriages dissolved, each moved back to the area, and they became reacquainted, having dated each other briefly in high school. The rest, they say, is history.

Since John's nightmare, he had remained pleasant and friendly, but I felt something had changed between us. He was much more reserved, and I worried that he thought I'd seen him in a different light and formed a new impression of him. That, of course, was absolutely not the case, and every time I wanted to mention it, I just couldn't seem to bring it up. So, we just avoided talking about it entirely.

Colette and her husband decided to make a night of it at the Inn. She packed a picnic dinner and some board games, something they both enjoyed, and they arrived just before we needed to leave. I was dressed and ready in a light pink, strapless, chiffon dress. I wore silver sandals with stacked heels on my feet, and only diamond drop earrings. With Audrey Hepburn as my style icon, I believed simple was best. I straightened my hair, and I braided the front, adding a silver clip with a rhinestone star on it that I found in Nana's box. My mother would be immensely pleased—I was tanner than I'd been in a couple of years, and there was color in my cheeks.

John knocked on my door to see if I was ready. When I opened it, I could tell by his expression that he approved of the way I looked. In fact, neither one of us had ever seen the other dressed formally. We wore working clothes at the Inn, which included lots of shorts and t-shirts, except for afternoon tea when I would wear a sundress or skirt and top. However, seeing him in the doorway with the sunlight illuminating him from the back made me pause. His light-colored suit was fitted perfectly, his tie a pastel blue with thin, pink stripes. I remembered Colette telling me he'd asked her what color my dress was, and now I knew why. He looked very handsome with his sun-tanned, high cheekbones and trimmed hair.

"You look stunning," he said.

In all the years I'd been with Gil, "stunning" was not a word he had ever used. "Beautiful," "pretty," "cute," and "adorable," may have been said numerous times over the years, but the word stunning with regard to my looks never crossed his lips.

"You look...do people still use the word 'dapper?'" I asked.

"Writers probably do," he said. "I'll take it. Dapper works. Makes me sound like Cary Grant."

"Ok, good, because you look very dapper, and you're kind of suave like Cary Grant."

"Really?" he said, his smile broadening. He seemed pleased to hear that. "That's a compliment I haven't received before—ever. I'll take it."

I winked at him and closed the cottage door behind me, silver glitter purse in hand, and John opened the car door for me. Proper manners. I was always a sucker for that. There's something old-fashioned and sweet about a man's attentive and good manners. My own father has the best manners and always treats my mother, my sister, and me with great respect.

We drove directly to the Oaks Waterfront Inn, which was technically between St. Michaels and Easton with a mailing address of Royal Oak, Maryland. Like Inn Significant, it was a waterfront property. Set back off a windy road on a cove, it also had a venue for hosting weddings and events. The wedding ceremony and cocktails were scheduled to take place on the lawn near the water, and the reception would be hosted inside in the banquet room with large windows looking out to the cove. The inn was lovely, and yet it was a completely different feel from our quaint Inn Significant.

Guests were being seated for the ceremony, and we were led

by a gentleman named Bud, someone John knew, who escorted us to our seats. Guests were facing the water in two sections of white chairs separated by an aisle, with flower garland strung across them. There was a trellis in the center where the bride and groom would stand, clematis and its purple and pink flowers dressing it up. When it was time for the ceremony to begin, the groom and his best man waited under the trellis for the bride to come down the aisle. It always amazes me just how beautiful women look on their wedding day. I remembered Gil saying that no woman ever looked lovelier than on that day. He was right; Mona was a beaming bride, in a tasteful, fitted tea-length gown. Its bodice had a sweetheart neckline and a sheer top and sleeves above the bustline with embroidered white flowers. It was cinched at the waist, and opened to a full-skirted bottom with crinoline. It was finished off with a pillbox hat and short veil netting atop her dark, raven hair and her porcelain skin. All I could think was that Audrey Hepburn would have been pleased. I wondered if we secretly had the same style icon. I admired, and often tried to emulate, Hepburn's fashion sense myself. Mona looked enchanting.

Greg was a good-looking man, as well. He had a lot of grey in his hair, but he had hair, which made him look distinguished. He was in a tan wedding suit with a white shirt and matching tan tie. He wore a single white rose boutonniere on his lapel. He was festively attired for a waterfront, outdoor wedding, and the pair of them couldn't have looked happier, more contented, or lovelier than they did standing under that trellis of flowers. Although I had never met John's friends before, when I saw them looking at each other and smiling, preparing to say their vows, I reached for my cellphone and snapped a picture of that sentimental moment.

John reached into his pocket and pulled out a handkerchief for me as I started to become teary. It was expected, right? While it was beautiful and tender, it also reminded me of my own wedding day just fifteen years ago. I felt a sunken feeling, a feeling of remorse. John must have sensed that I was reminiscing because he gently placed his hand on my thigh and gave it a light squeeze as if to say he was here and everything was all right. He turned his head slightly and gave me a little smile.

I was thankful for that moment and won't ever forget it.

*

The romantic aspect of weddings is how much love and affection floats around the room. As we moved inside for dinner and dancing, the place was bustling with the noise of music and people talking, and it wasn't difficult to observe what was occurring. As I only knew one person there, it was easy for me to be a spectator and watch and interpret the actions of those in the room. Guests kissed, hugged, and smiled. Therefore, as the observer, it was difficult to be melancholy at a wedding when it was plain to see how much two people felt love for the other. Their joy was contagious, and guests wanted to cling to that love euphoria as they danced, drank Champagne, and ate food and cake.

John and I danced. The first song that got us on the dance floor was *In My Life* by The Beatles, one of Greg's favorites that he requested. Feeling John's hand on the small of my back, the warmth of it, his other hand holding my own was a bit confusing. I both liked it and it made me feel uncomfortable. I liked feeling close to him, but my mind kept telling me it was wrong.

"You're a good dancer," John said, looking me in the eyes, a sweet smile running across his face.

"Thanks," I said, "you too."

"If you added up all the time people spend dancing, I'd probably say that collectively, we should do more of it."

"You mean all these people in the room should collectively dance?" I asked, trying to keep things light.

"Yes. Let's invite them all over later for some more dancing," he teased.

My husband was dead, I was dancing with another man, and by the sound of our exchange, I seemed to be flirting with him, too.

How could I be enjoying dancing with another man? When the song ended, I hurried back to the table, and sat down. I sipped my glass of wine.

"Are you okay, Milly?" he asked me.

"Yes, great," I said, although I could sense he didn't believe me.

Thankfully, Greg and Mona were making their rounds to each of the tables, and ours was next. We both waved to them and smiled, and within a couple of minutes they came over to us, arms extended. They hugged us and thanked us profusely for sharing their day.

"Your dress and whole look is so gorgeous," I told her.

"Thank you, Milly. You look so pretty as well. Love this pink dress."

"Inspired by Audrey," I said, seeing if she caught on to the reference.

"Me, too! Audrey head to toe!" she exclaimed, and we laughed. "John has told me so much about you, I feel as if I know you already. We have to get together, the four of us, and do something fun. Maybe we can go boating and have a couple's day out and get to know one another."

She considered us an item, which we were not. We were being referred to as a couple. Mona was sweet as can be, but she was under the wrong impression. I didn't correct her, though. I didn't think it was the right thing to do on her wedding day, and I certainly didn't want her to feel awkward about anything she said later. No. I kept my mouth shut and smiled.

Greg and John were having a conversation about high school, fishing, and how the Orioles were playing this season. I kept watching the two of them interact out of the corner of my eye to see if Greg made any references or inferences to us being a couple, too. I didn't sense any sort of relationship talk was taking place, so I focused back on Mona and asked where they were going for their honeymoon.

The uneasy truth was, I found the whole act of going on a date to a wedding with someone an intimate endeavor. You wouldn't necessarily go with just anyone—you would most likely attend a wedding with someone you were interested in dating seriously, or at least someone you wanted to get to know better. The reason for this theory was simple: there was just so much romance in the air, and it was often contagious. As I was trying to further elaborate on this theory, I started to laugh to myself. I realized I had the propensity to overthink things to a fault, which was most likely what I had just done. I was trying to talk myself out of the moment. It was either that, or it was the wine talking.

*

The drive back to the Inn was quiet. We chatted a little bit about the cake and the funny toast the best man made. I'm not quite sure exactly what was happening, but when we parked the car at the Inn, John opened my door for me, and we walked to our cottages in silence. He walked me all the way up to the front door where I'd left the light on.

"Thank you for taking me to the wedding," I said. "I had a nice time."

"Thank you for going," he said, and he reached for my hand and took it in his, turned it over, and took it to his lips and kissed it. "Are you sure you're okay?" he asked again.

"Yes. I'm fine," I said. "I'll see you in the morning."

His eyes met mine, and I smiled.

"Goodnight, Milly," he said.

"Goodnight, John."

I stepped inside the cottage and closed the door, leaning my back up against it and looking around. I caught a glimpse of the photo of Gil and me sitting on the Spanish Steps in Italy. It's one of my favorite photos, not because of the way we looked that day, but because of what we felt that day: complete and utter relaxation and just the splendor of being together. We had asked a stranger to take the photo, and somehow he captured the essence of the moment perfectly. I was content in Gil's arms, in Rome, among the history, inhaling another culture—its food and its people. We were connected by yet another experience filled with inside jokes and reverie for a place that exuded romance out of every historical crevice, curvy street, and marvelously pungent restaurant.

That moment. Click. There it was.

Not everyone was as lucky as I was to have a photograph like that. There are some moments we can't capture on film or digitally, because we're outside the moment and not living in the moment. Of all the photos I have of the two of us, that's the one I would save if a fire ravaged the place. That's the one I would want to keep forever. That's the one that would be in my box, and just as Nana had a box of things that reminded her of Ferio, I had one gem that reminded me of Gil.

Ferio.

Thinking his name made me realize I had to get back to my reading. That's how I would spend the next hour...reading before sleep. I changed out of my pink dress and into my pajamas, washed my face, brushed my teeth, and crawled between the cool sheets with Nana's words on my lap.

12 June 1933

It's been a wonderful week. Ferio has been at home and not working on the boat. He was feeling ill for the first day, but soon became well again. I like to take the credit for curing him because I cooked a delicious meal and rubbed his feet and read to him. We spent the days in the garden or taking walks by the water. We made a picnic lunch and took it to the park, where we stretched our legs on a blanket and talked of plans for the future. He told me not to worry about my problems conceiving a child—that it would happen when God believed it was the right time for us. Whenever Ferio mentions God, I know he is speaking from the heart, because although he doesn't always attend church, he is an incredibly spiritual and blessed man. I told Ferio he was right—that it would happen in time, and that perhaps the fact that he is now home will help relax me about this particular issue.

I know I haven't gone into great detail about how deeply I love this man, but it is the most beautiful love I could ever imagine. There is never any doubt about how much Ferio loves me; I know he loves me with every ounce of his soul and that he and I are intertwined so wholly that nothing could ever tear us apart. When he looks at me with those dark eyes, I am his. I want nothing more than his arms around me holding me tightly and to feel his soft kisses on my cheeks and lips. I yearn to see his beaming smile.

I am so grateful that he and I found each other in this great big world. I thank God every day for him.

I found myself sniffling after those last few sentences. I reached for the photo of Italy and stared at it again, bringing it closer to my face. He was perfect. He was my Gil. He was everything to me, and just as Nana said about Ferio, I longed for his kisses and to feel his arms wrapped around me. I still ached with pain when I thought that I would never see him again in this lifetime.

How fragile life is. How the moments of our lives could vacillate and be euphoric, unpredictable, sullen, maddening, and sorrowful.

I examined Gil's eyes in the photo, struggling to remember all the expressions they could make, the stories they could tell, and all the love that was behind every glance, look, and stare. At some point, I fell asleep with the open journal on top of the covers, and awakened to find myself still clutching the photo in my hands.

CHAPTER 16

It was Sunday morning and I was having a difficult time getting myself going. Colette was already in the kitchen making the breakfast when I arrived, and I felt badly that she worked seven mornings a week. I was determined to take some of that burden away from her, but she didn't seem to mind. She said it gave her a sense of purpose.

"You know John's birthday is tomorrow, right?"

"What? No, I didn't. Oh, gosh. What should we do for him?"

"Well, I was thinking we should get him that little kayak he wants."

"What kayak?" I asked, bewildered. He hadn't said anything to me about a kayak.

"The one in that magazine he showed me," she said.

"He didn't show me," I said. "Do you know which magazine?"

"Not off hand. He was walking around with it two days ago and was showing it to me. I think he's pretty excited about it. The one he wants costs about $250. I'd sure be willing to pitch in."

"I would, too. And I'm sure my parents would as well. But how can we find out which exact one he wants?"

"Do you have a key to his cottage? I bet the magazine is in

there."

"The Inn's office has a key to his cottage. Do you want me to sneak in? I've never stepped a foot inside it."

"Is that so?" Colette teased.

"I swear to you. I've never been inside. Has he gone for his morning run?"

"Yes," Colette said. "And he just left about ten minutes ago."

*

I turned the key to his cottage, looking left and right before entering, hoping that he wouldn't catch me. I stepped inside and closed the door behind me. His cottage was neat as a pin, and it smelled like him—clean and manly. I walked into his living area, and spotted the magazine Colette was mentioning; it was folded open to the exact page with a yellow sticky note on it as a tab. As I walked over to it, I caught a glimpse of something entirely unexpected next to his desk. An easel, art supplies, sketchbooks and papers, and piles of drawings and sketches.

The desk and easels were covered with artwork of all kinds, and I found myself compelled to look at them, even though it felt a great deal like snooping. But I couldn't help myself. There were scenes of war, a sketch of a man in military attire, drawings of the Inn and the river, a watercolor of Plane To Sea, John's boat. There were also watercolors of landscapes. I couldn't believe my eyes. They were all signed or initialed JS—John Salvie. The art was stunning in its own right, and some were so lifelike and incredible that all I could think was that they needed to be displayed somewhere for people to see and appreciate his amazing talent. Granted, I knew little about art, but I knew when I saw something incredible, and it was all so moving. There was something about the way the paintings and illustrations reflected what he saw in people—vivid, raw emotion and expressions that were captivating.

I snapped a picture with my phone of the ad for the kayak in the magazine so I didn't have to take it and cause him to suspect anything. I wanted to leave before John got back and found me rummaging through his masterpieces, though part of me didn't want to leave at all, but rather stay and look at more of his work. I put everything back exactly as it was and snuck out the door before he returned.

Karen hung the key back on the rack for me and promised not to breathe a word of my secret break-in. She laughed and called me Sherlock Holmes. I told her she could only call me that if I actually got the kayak. It would be a miracle if I could pull off a big gift like that in a day.

Within minutes, I was on the office phone with Easton Cycle and Sports asking them if they had the model John was interested in purchasing. They asked me to hold the line. When the salesperson returned to the phone, he said, "Good news," and I began reciting my credit card number into the receiver and arranging delivery for first thing in the morning.

Just as I left the office to go to the kitchen and tell Colette I got the job done, John came running through the gates sweating from his run, slowing to a walk, and pacing back and forth to cool himself down. Dressed in Under Armour from head to toe, he was in great shape, that was for sure, but today, the day before his thirty-eighth birthday, I stopped and took the time to look at him. Really look at him. I was feeling incredibly shallow that I hadn't tried harder to get to know him better and realized that the guilt I harbored for outliving my husband was holding me back from everything—from friendship, from love, and from making a new life.

The truth was, waking up and clinging to Gil's picture in my hands was never going to bring him back.

*

On the third ring, I was about to hang up, when Angela picked up her cell phone. "I noticed your number...how are you?" she said breathlessly as she answered.

"Good, sort of," I said.

"I haven't heard from you in a while, so I was hoping everything was going well for you, Milly."

"It is," I said, knowing how precious her time was and that she was being kind by talking with me over the phone. "There is such a thing as feeling guilty about living—about being alive—when you're husband's dead, right? I mean, I'm having difficulty allowing myself to move forward, with people—"

"You've met someone," she said.

"I've known him peripherally for a couple of years," I said. "And he's very nice. Only he and I both have issues with the past. He was in the military and served overseas and witnessed horrible things. But it's bigger than that. It's scary to form attachments, you know?"

"I do. I know very well, but dwelling on the past gets us nowhere. Nowhere at all. And you can't protect yourself from hurt for the rest of your life. At some point, you're going to have to allow yourself to be vulnerable," she said.

"Thanks, Angela."

"You're welcome. And yes, your feelings are normal. You loved Gil. Anyone who loved someone that much is going to feel a whole host of emotions as you try to build a life without him."

"God, it's still so sad to me. I never thought I would have to build a life without him."

"No one ever does," Angela sighed. "But you may surprise us yet, Milly Foster. Anything is possible."

*

Colette was still cleaning up the breakfast mess when I told her that the kayak would be delivered in the morning, and she gave me a high-five.

"You pulled it off. Way to go!" she said.

Karen appeared in the doorway, a puzzled look on her face.

"What's the matter?" I asked her.

"Miles Channing wants a room for the night, but we're booked," she said. "I told him I would check with you, and that I would call him right back."

"Are you sure? I thought we had one room available. Let me come with you to the office."

Karen and I walked back together to check the books. I was the only one in the office earlier, and I took the cancellation call. In my morning stupor, I forgot to cross it off in the reservation book, as well as on the computer.

"This couple here—Ed and Fiona Drake—they cancelled early this morning before you got here. I'm sorry. I didn't do a good job of communicating that."

"So, there is a room?"

"Yes. Tell Mr. Channing there is a room for him at the Inn."

*

August was oppressively hot, with high humidity and scorching temperatures. My hair didn't take too kindly to the humidity, as it made it unmanageable, frizzy, and unusually big, reminiscent of the 1980s, without the teasing. I found myself wearing it up in a ponytail, braid, or even in a high bun. Muggy, heavy air choked us, and I walked the grounds that morning excited for the fall season to arrive next month. Unlike most kids, I was one who longed for school to start again. I loved looking forward to autumn, Halloween, and Thanksgiving . Going back to school meant I could shop for new clothes, see all my friends, and participate in activities I loved, especially in high school. For a year, I served as the editor of our literary magazine, something I adored because of our advisor, Mrs. Shelley. She was the one who truly made me love writing. Her free-flowing, inspirational classroom was filled with creativity—and we were permitted and encouraged to be as imaginative as possible, which she highly regarded. When it came time to apply for college, Mrs. Shelley wrote the most beautiful recommendation letter for me.

Oxford hummed during the
tors were staying in Oxford or St. I
often come for a morning or afterno
down the street, Mystery Loves Cor
it hosted authors for book talks, and c
bookstore earlier to see if they happened to have a book I wanted to
read to help me better understand some of the psychology of recent
war, and they did. There was a book that recalled one chaplain's two
tours of duty in Iraq as he helped soldiers cope with various aspects
of war. I thought reading a story told from his perspective might offer some insight on the subject.

"Where are you off to?" John asked, when he saw me hop-
ping on my bike.

"Just down to the bookstore. A book I requested is in and I
have to pick it up. Do you need anything from Oxford Market?" I
asked.

"Actually, yes. Would you mind getting me some Gatorade?
I'm all out."

"Happy to do it," I said.

It was so refreshing not to have to get into a car for every
little errand. While the Oxford Market was by no means large, and
we had a Safeway just a few miles away, I loved the idea of bik-
ing down the street to pick up little things we needed. The Market

d fresh pies and breads, and made fresh sandwiches. Co-
often stopped by the market in the mornings when we needed
fruit and pastries for breakfast. Housing a good selection of wines, I
wanted to purchase a bottle or two to toast John on his birthday and
a buy card for him that we could all sign as well.

After all of my goodies were piled up in my front and back
baskets, I began the ride back. A car pulled up next to me and the
driver shouted out the window—"Are you a good witch or a bad
witch?"

I got the reference immediately—Ms. Gulch in *The Wizard
of Oz* riding her bike. All I needed was Toto.

I waved and knew exactly to whom the wave was directed:
Miles Channing.

*

"I heard you were going to grace us with your presence again,"
I said as I walked my bike up near the office and put the kickstand
down.

"Gracing you with my presence—I like that," Miles said.
"Yes, here I am. Freaking tired, worn out from all this research I've
been doing, and I swear, if I have to talk to that tobacco farmer again,
I'm bringing you with me. Maybe you can get some good stuff out of

him."

"Well, you'll be happy to know you can relax here, put your feet up, have a glass of wine, and not be bothered by anyone if you like."

"I'd like to be bothered by you for a bit if you're free. Crabs at The Masthead at eight o'clock?"

There was no way to say "no" to Miles. And anyway, who would want to?

*

Karen was on late shift that night. She happened to see me exit my cottage wearing a skirt and a cotton blouse with silver, beaded sandals. She raised her eyebrows in an all-knowing, "I can keep a secret," girls-understand-girls sort of way, and I smirked back at her. Miles met me on the lawn, and I called to Karen, "I've got my phone if you need me." She gave me the "OK" sign and vanished into the office.

"You're looking well," Miles said, as he pecked me on the cheek.

"You as well," I said.

It was a short walk to the restaurant, and we both agreed that even though it was still incredibly muggy, it was summer after all, so we took advantage of an evening stroll to dinner. Miles was tanner than the last time I saw him, and he wore army-green cargo shorts and a fitted, black Metallica t-shirt.

"I didn't peg you for a heavy metal lover."

"Oh, no? Yes. Huge fan, but I do love all kinds of music, including the Rolling Stones, the Zac Brown Band, and even the Black Eyed Peas, for workouts primarily, of course. However, my Sinatra collection is enviable."

"If you like Sinatra," I teased.

"Blasphemy! Do you not like Sinatra?"

"Everyone likes Sinatra. And Buble."

"Ah, yes. The modern Sinatra. He's okay. But not the real thing."

"But he's his own real thing. I saw him live. He was terrific," I said, referring to the concert Gil and I attended in Washington, D.C. at Verizon Center shortly before Gil's death. Buble was a showman with his deep voice and raunchy, silly sense of humor. Those were the days when I laughed a lot.

"Ok, I'll give you Buble, and you leave me with Sinatra."

"Fair deal," I said. "By the way, thank you so much for helping me with the research you found on my grandmother. It was very helpful. I took a picture of the house she lived in on Bank Street. The woman who lives there now was the sweetest thing. She found an old box in her crawl space that contained items my grandmother had saved, including a couple of photos of her with Ferio, her first husband. It's the first time I got to see what he looked like."

"Wow. You may very well be a better investigative reporter than I am. I may need to enlist your help."

"Keep on flattering me, Miles. I think I like it."

"I think I just may," he said with a laugh.

When we were seated at the table on the water, we ordered two salads, a dozen crabs, and corn-on-the-cob. It was a little cooler on the water with the gentle breeze blowing, offering us a little bit of circulated air. The sun was beginning to set, and I found myself enjoying, once again, Miles' company. He was a talker, somewhat smooth, but very engaging; he knew just how to look you in the eye and involve you in the conversation. With some people, I never felt as if I were actually part of the conversation. That was not the case with Miles. He knew how to listen. He knew how to make you feel you mattered.

"So, what I really want to know is what you're going to do about all this stuff you're discovering," Miles said.

"What stuff?"

"Your grandmother's journal, the history you are uncovering about her life and about hubby number one. What do you plan on doing with it?"

"What should I be doing with it?"

"You should be writing it, of course. Write a story."

"I have to admit to you, I actually haven't finished reading her journal yet. It's cumbersome and her handwriting is a challenge, but I'm getting through it little by little. What if there is no story?"

"But there is, don't you see? I would bet my mortgage—even though it's a small one—that by the end of that discovery, you will have some sort of marvelous story to tell."

"How are you so confident?" I asked, honestly wanting to know how he could be so secure in this notion.

"Because everybody has a story, Milly," he said. "Some are just told better than others."

*

After dinner and our walk back, I found myself standing at the Inn under the light of the moon with Miles. We'd been gone for almost three hours, and we both caught ourselves yawning, not out of boredom, but because we were both exhausted and full from dinner and a couple of drinks.

"So if everybody has a story, what's your story, Miles? Is there someone special in your life?"

"I'll never tell," he said.

"Or are there lots of special people in your life?"

"Are you asking me if I have a significant other or lots of significant others?"

"I think that's what I'm asking."

"I probably lean more toward the latter. Went through a wicked-ass divorce several years ago, and I've never really been inclined to go down that path again. I'm too busy. I travel all the time. No chance of me setting down roots now, and it doesn't leave room for any sort of successful long-term relationship. But friendship, I've got lots of room for that," he said.

"I'm not looking for a romantic relationship either," I said. "Too painful."

"Maybe not right now, but eventually you will. And you don't want to become a cynic like me and endure casual relationships with casual sex. There are little redeeming qualities to it, but it works for me now, as callous as that sounds."

There it was. Miles was still hurt and had become hardened—and a playboy. I pictured a woman in every town he visited. It was okay because I knew what he was saying, and I understood that we all cope with our feelings differently. I liked Miles, he was attractive, but I knew he was not someone with whom I could ever become involved. He was a sort of a nomad, flying by the seat of his pants, and that wasn't the type of relationship I could ever see ex-

ploring, although he was incredibly charming. It was a relief to know
we could be friends and flirt and nothing would become of it. There
was great comfort in that. We heard the sounds of an owl and looked
at each other, grinning.

"Whooooo knows, Miles. You may fall madly in love again,"
I teased.

"Your attempt at humor, I see. Enough about me and my
putrid love life. As for you, I get the impression that you're still reeling and vulnerable. But you are so ready to move beyond that, don't
you think? I think you've been tragically sad—and rightfully so—for
long enough. As one of your newest, bluntest friends, I'm suggesting
you do yourself a favor: write a little bit. Do it for yourself, if for no
one else. Or, do it for me. It's as therapeutic as anything else you can
do."

I looked at this man I didn't know too well, but with whom I
felt such an immediate connection. "I promise. After I finish reading
Nana's journal, I will set aside some time to write something. I don't
know what, but I promise it will be something."

"Good. Even if you just show it to me. Deal?"

"Deal," I said.

"Or, you can share the story you write on your website, which
looks five hundred times better, by the way."

"You saw it?"

"Um…you should know me a little bit by now. I dissected it. I think it looks fantastic. What did Mom and Dad say?"

"They were very pleased by it," I said. "But even more so because my sister and I created it together. She's the technical person."

"Well, you both did wonders. Keep it up. Maybe you'll finally have a first blog post to write from the Inn."

"Maybe," I said.

"I'll probably be gone early tomorrow—got to meet the farmer again at six in the morning to see some of his great grandfather's machinery. It was the only time he would do it. I won't make you come with me," he said, teasingly.

He took a step closer to me, then leaned in and kissed me—one soft, quick, kiss on the cheek.

"Thanks for a great night," he said, and he began his walk up to the Inn. I watched him go for a second and then turned and walked back to my quiet, empty cottage.

*

There was no way I would be able to sleep. Miles got me thinking about Nana, Ferio, the journal, and writing. It made me wonder if I missed it enough to pursue that career again. I associated my love for journalism and writing with Gil. He was the one who read every one of my stories, offered suggestions when I suffered from writer's block, and loved hearing about the interviews I conducted, the people I met, and the places I visited. He would always say, "You try being stuck in an office all day—you don't know how lucky you are to talk to people and explore the world," even if my little world was the Washington metropolitan area and surrounding counties. Gil lived vicariously through my articles, and there was no question he was my biggest supporter. When I first told my parents I wanted to be a writer, they were worried I'd never make enough money to eat, let alone afford a place to live. But once I got that first internship, things began to change, and they saw me take my writing career seriously. But it was Gil who always pushed me.

I thought of him now as I opened Nana's journal, remembering the way he would tell me to "soldier on" when I came to an impasse when writing. "If anyone can do it, you can," he would tell me. I sat in the stillness of the cottage in the white chair next to the tall lamp, and began to allow the echoes of Nana's voice to fill the void of silence.

15 July 1933

Once again, I am without a child, and both Ferio and I long not to feel the sadness of disappointment. After I lost this one, I became unusually sad, which I had promised I would not do again the last time this happened.

This is the third pregnancy lost, and I am not sure I can take much more. I long to have a little darling in my arms, one that looks like my husband with all of his goodness and kindness. As is typical of my husband, Ferio pampered me when I delivered the news by simply loving me, kissing me, and telling me how much he loves me. For the next two days, he took great care of me, tried to lift my spirits with fresh flowers from the garden and walks to the river, and we even listened to a radio program I loved far more than he did. But he did these things for me. I will always love him for his caring ways. I will keep praying that someday we will have a child together. I do so long for that moment.

Her entries during the month of August sounded as if times were more stressful. She mentioned lost wages and the struggles of the townspeople. I kept reading until I got to the end of August, and when I finished reading the next journal entry, I wished I had never read it.

30 August 1933

I have faithfully written in this journal, sharing my thoughts and my life with Ferio. I never dreamed I would have to write and tell the following story, but I feel I must.

The Great Hurricane of 1933 arrived August 23 and pummeled the East Coast through August 24.

I was staying with friends in Easton in a brick house away from the water during the frightful storm. I was too afraid to stay in the Oxford house alone, and I didn't know when Ferio would return. My heart raced the entire time, and I worried for his safety. The rain hammered down upon us and nearly eight inches fell, flooding our town. The storm surge levels were measured at an all-time high, the newspaper said.

There were advanced warnings for the state regarding the imminent horrible weather predicted for the East Coast; Ferio knew conditions were worsening, and he and his men attempted to get back into port. The churning tide of the Chesapeake was brewing and they struggled to get the boat ashore. As the waves were intensifying, Ferio was tossed inside the boat, tossed so hard, that he was thrown off the ship and submerged in the water. His head hit the edge of the vessel. One of his shipmates had saved him, but he was knocked unconscious and sent to the hospital.

After the storm had passed and I returned home to the house in Oxford, I received word about Ferio. Apparently, his shipmates had tried to track me down, but most folks had vacated the area; no one knew where I was. When they told me the story, I immediately went to the hospital. I was trembling and desperately afraid. When I arrived, the doctor told me about the horrible blow Ferio suffered to his head, and they were worried that he had other internal injuries as well. The doctors were worried about his brain, as he had not regained consciousness since the accident.

According to the doctor, nothing could be done, and so I sat and held his hand and sang him songs and cried and kissed his hand and held him the best I could. I knew instinctively that something was severely wrong… that he would not wake up…that he would no longer talk to me and smile…that we would never again laugh together. That my world as I knew it was over.

Ferio died two nights later. I was holding his hand when I heard his last breath and secretly wished it were also my last.

My family arrived for the funeral a couple of days later. It was nothing much to speak of, but I did host some of his shipmates and my family afterwards at our home, and my mother stayed with me and let me cry on her shoulders into the wee hours of the morning.

I expected the depression to ruin us all, not an unwelcomed, frightening hurricane. I expected to live a long life with Ferio by my side. There was no doubt that I worried for his safety every time he was on a ship, and now I know that that worry was not unfounded. However, to me, Ferio was invincible, as was our love. Despite my nervousness about his safety, I thought we would grow old together.

How incredibly wrong I was. How I took everything for granted…

CHAPTER 17

I was still up when I heard Miles start his car and drive away early in the morning. It was John's birthday, the kayak would arrive in a few hours, and I hadn't slept a wink. The thought of my grandmother losing the love of her life was too much for me to bear as I listened to the clock on the wall tick away. It was like losing Gil all over again. Somehow, I felt her presence in the room that night. Hearing her words about Ferio made realize for the first time since Gil's death that I was not alone. Many people in the world suffered losses. I was not an anomaly. I'd been selfish in that approach to grief.

And yet, when tragedy happens to you, you do feel as if you are the only person in the world who has experienced great pain and loss. My grandmother suffered the same. Clearly, she loved Ferio as much as I loved Gil. She suffered a loss that left her feeling alone in the world. Her family was miles away, and she was still in Oxford. She refused to leave what had become her home and struggled to carry on.

As I continued to read entry after entry, I learned just how many challenges my grandmother faced during her young life. She managed somehow to survive on a tailor and dressmaker's salary as the depression era continued. She began making essential items to sell in the local clothier's shop for the winter months, such as scarves, mittens, and hats. She went on to become an active member of the

Church of the Holy Trinity, helping to organize church events. She persevered, and as she wrote in an entry from June of 1934, *I carry on in good faith because that's what Ferio would have wanted for me. He would not have wanted me to live in a perpetual state of sadness.*

I read all one-hundred and twenty entries she wrote after Ferio's death; mostly they were about the loneliness and the trials she faced, but she clearly turned to God for help, stating at one point, *He is the best listener; God is always there for me whenever I need a sturdy chat or to shed a few tears.*

The respect I gained for her after reading those particular writings was tantamount to the lessons I learned from her when she was here with us. She was only in her twenties then, but hearing her sage, rational voice had a poignancy that left me missing her and wishing I could speak to her about Ferio, her loss, and moving on. I felt even closer to her now than I did when she was alive because we shared similar fates, even if they were not welcome fates.

A couple of hours later, after dozing a bit and still curled up in the chair, there was loud rapping on my door. "Milly—are you there? Milly?"

I wanted to curl up under my covers and hide from the world. The thought of having to engage in pleasant conversation was too much for me. The knocking did not go away, and as John was saying my name, with each utterance of it, I heard his tone change from one of happiness to real concern. I was left with no choice but to go and open the door before I worried everyone.

"Coming," I finally said.

I opened the door in my pajamas with the white cotton blanket still wrapped around my shoulders. I must have looked dreadful because the trepidation in John's eyes could not be disguised.

"I'm sorry—did I wake you?" he asked gently.

"No—" I began to say, and I noticed he was trying to look inside the cottage, perhaps to see if anyone was with me.

"Are you okay?"

"Long night," I said. "Happy birthday!" It took every ounce of energy I had to try to make myself sound enthusiastic. I reached up and gave him a quick hug.

"Thank you for the kayak. It was just delivered. It's very cool! Do you want to take it out with me? I think you deserve the first ride."

I almost said no, and then I got a glimpse of the day, the sunshine, the greenness of the grass, the vibrant red roses along the white picket fence, the glint in John's eyes—a glimmer of childlike happiness in them—and I heard Nana's words in my head: *I carry on in good faith because that's what Ferio would have wanted for me. He would not have wanted me to live in a state of perpetual sadness.*

"Give me a few minutes to get myself together?"

"Take all the time you need," he said. "Whenever you're ready, I'll be waiting."

*

The river was calm, and the kayak glided along the water as both John and I guided it with our paddles. There were quite a few boats out, and we rowed together gently, listening to the sounds of our paddles as they hit the water and splashed. A few silver fish jumped, and a baby turtle's head was peeking out of the river until he saw us draw nearer, and then he disappeared under the water. The sun was hot—steamy—but we created our own breeze from the movement of the kayak, so it felt wonderful. There was something incredibly freeing about being on the water. Perhaps that's what Ferio loved about it, too.

The last few days felt like a whirlwind to me, from attending the wedding with John to having dinner with Miles to reading Nana's haunting words on the pages. I was trying my best to follow Angela's steadfast advice—live in the moment— the best that I could, but my mind was now full of questions, emotions, and still, the lingering effects of guilt. Nana's story was not over; there was still a whole new life she led to uncover. How did she meet Grandpa? How did she ultimately let go of Ferio? How was she able to move on?

Now obsessively engrossed in her story, I wanted desperately to talk to my mother. I'd only shared bits and pieces of the story with her so far because she insisted that she wanted to read the journal herself. But I was missing her now more than I had since she left for Ireland.

"So, are you going to tell me what kept you awake all night or is it going to be the elephant in the room?" John asked, breaking the silence and taking me away from my thoughts.

"It was Nana's journal," I said. "I found out what happened to Ferio and how he died. It was very tragic."

"I'm sorry," was all John said. We listened to the birds chirping and heard the sounds of the powerboat that soared past us going much too fast. The wake of the boat caused us to rock a bit, and we both hoisted up our paddles and allowed the kayak to bounce and float along without help. When the waves dissipated, we began to row again, and as we moved around toward the Inn, we could see Colette standing at the water's edge waving to us. We both called to her and waved back, and I realized how lucky I was at that moment to be surrounded by the kindness of others—Karen, Darlene, Colette, and John—four people who made me feel nothing but welcome from the first day I arrived and who never complained about any of their tasks. They were genuinely good, honest, decent people, working hard to offer our guests the best possible experience at the

Inn, and I was so indebted to them for their help and guidance in keeping the Inn running smoothly.

*

That evening, after I napped for an hour and afternoon tea was over, Colette came back to the Inn at six o'clock. She prepared a feast for John's birthday. The wine was chilling on ice, and we all signed the card for his birthday. We pushed the two outdoor picnic tables together, and dressed them with white linens, flowers from the garden in glass vases, and votive candles. We strung white party lights from the two nearby trees that added to the ambiance.

After the kayak ride earlier, I snuck into the office, found the phone number for John's parents, and invited them to dine with us for his birthday. They were flattered by the invitation and excited to come, and they offered to pick up John's grandmother, Violette, from her assisted living residence, as well. I was genuinely looking forward to meeting them. Darlene and her husband, Vic, and Colette and her husband, Mark, and Karen would be there along with me to celebrate his birthday.

"My goodness! Did you cook up a storm!" I said to Colette when I saw the amount of food she prepared.

"I figured since we're eating dinner al fresco we'd do a whole

Tuscan, Italian-themed dinner."

"It looks incredible—and we all know how much John loves pasta," I said.

"And olives," Colette teased, making a reference to the time John ate a whole can of olives that she needed for an afternoon tea salad she was preparing. The salad was prepared that day without olives in it, not that anyone knew they were supposed to be in it except us.

I helped Colette carry everything outside. Karen was helping, too, and we set the antipasto—the bruschetta, fresh cantaloupe and prosciutto, and small olive platter—on the table. Karen pulled out her iPhone and took a photo.

"What are you doing with that?" I asked her.

"It's too pretty not to put it on Instagram," she said, and she was right. Lately, I hadn't taken any new photos for the website. With the gardens changing and brightening with August's bursts of color, I should have been more on top of it. And maybe the picture of the tables would inspire the perfect first blog post, since I had yet to write one. So, following Karen's lead, I reached into my back pocket, grabbed my own cellphone, and snapped a photo, adjusting the angle to allow the perfect light to stream through the trees so that the image would showcase the elaborate birthday feast properly.

I ran back to the cottage to change. I slipped into a strapless, white, cotton dress and my sparkly sandals. The humidity had dissipated, so I straightened my hair and let it down. I added a little mascara, blush, and pink lipstick. I looked down at my hands. They were tan and naked, as I stopped wearing my wedding ring on New Year's Day, my own little resolution to myself. It had to happen at some point. It was tucked away in my jewelry box, though I knew I would probably never wear it again.

When I heard commotion outside as John's parents arrived with Violette, I checked myself in the mirror one last time. There were butterflies in my stomach, mostly because I wanted the party to be successful for John's sake, and also because I wanted to make a good impression on his parents and grandmother.

John was surprised to see them, and I caught up to them as he walked his family down toward the picnic tables; the sun was still up and the trees offered the perfect amount of shade for dining. I said hello to them, and John stopped and properly introduced me.

"Mom, Dad, Grandma—this is Milly Foster, the newest inn-keeper who is filling in for her parents for the year," he said.

"Temporary innkeeper," I said with a smile. "My previous 'unemployed' status made it easy for my parents to put me to work at the Inn for a bit."

"Well, the Inn is lucky to have you," Violette said. "You're the spitting image of your mother, and she is just the dearest. I miss seeing her on bridge nights."

"Thank you so much," I said. "She is the best. But so is your grandson. I don't know what I would do without him here."

Violette smiled and grabbed my hand. "I think he feels the same, dear," she said, and I saw John begin to blush.

"Okay, let's get to the table. I think Colette's cooking is going to be the biggest treat of the night," he said to Violette, trying to change the subject.

Everyone was already there, and Colette was pouring glasses of wine for everyone. Her husband, Mark, was a kind and thoughtful man. He was always smiling, and it was easy to see how much he adored his wife.

When we all settled at the table, I was across from John, his parents on either side of him, and his grandmother sat next to me. She wasn't at all what I expected; she had a sturdy, yet petite build, and she looked at least ten years younger than her age. She carried a cane for stability, she said, but she rarely used it. Her hair was short, in a sort of pixie cut, and she was sharp as a tack. And if I were not mistaken, I believe John was the apple of her eye. I could see the way she doted on him.

John's parents were delightful, upbeat people. His father's skin was leathery, but there was a twinkle in his blue eyes that offset his silver grey hair. His mother was very thin, with high cheekbones, and a pin-straight bob that was colored a blondish-red. I could tell they were pleased to be among all of us celebrating John, and when it came time for the toast, it was Colette who began.

"Before we start the antipasto, I just want to say what a delight it is to work here, to be with these people every day, and how much we love having John around. The Inn has never looked so beautiful—just look at the gardens—and Milly and I even talked John into growing food in the big food garden over there. So, on his very young, thirty-eighth birthday, we say thank you to John who helped us grow this basil, along with other herbs, that are flavoring your food tonight. Cheers to John and well wishes for many more birthdays surrounded by those who love you."

John decided to speak and respond. "Thank you for all this hard work, Colette," John said. "And thank you all for being here. I appreciate it so much."

"Cheers," everyone said, as they raised their glasses.

*

Colette's lemon spaghetti with fresh basil, the grilled eggplant Parmesan, asparagus with shaved sharp provolone, and citrus salmon satisfied all of our palates. We passed the platters, along with the bread from the Oxford Market, and Karen and I took turns taking group shots of all of us at the table as we dined.

As the night wore on, we passed the wine and our bellies became full, we exchanged stories of Oxford, of growing up or spending time in the town. We talked about the restaurants, which were the best and which ones we missed, the Creamery and how delicious the ice cream was, and about how living near the water gives one a sense of peace. We discussed the tourists and how they always describe the place as "quaint," and we all seemed thankful to just be with each other that night, sharing the joy of John's birthday celebration.

I can honestly say without hesitation that I was truly and unabashedly living in the moment. Then, everything changed.

*

Everyone was still laughing and having a good time at the table, when I decided to go inside and get the cake. As I approached the Inn, Karen and John were huddled together on the front porch, both of them having excused themselves to use the restroom. I could tell they were deep in conversation, and they hadn't seen me, so I stood back, wondering what they were talking about in those hushed tones. I caught a piece of the conversation.

"I think you should just tell her instead of running away

from it," I heard Karen say.

"I can't," he said. "It's not the right time. I thought maybe the wedding would be a chance—"

She interrupted him. "And now you think you shouldn't stay? I think you're wrong, but you'll think and do what you want," Karen said. "Why are men so pig-headed? Why do you think you can run away from your problems?"

The conversation was confusing; it was also almost laughable that a twenty-one-year-old was giving a thirty-eight-year-old man advice about women. I didn't want to hear any more. I snuck around to the back kitchen door instead of going through the porch so they wouldn't know I heard part of their conversation. Immediately, I hated myself for eavesdropping, and I wasn't sure if I understood the whole context of the conversation. My stomach dropped, and yet somehow I wondered if I needed to correct whatever impressions I made with John at the wedding that may have hurt his feelings. Was I so closed off I couldn't even allow our friendship to grow?

Was he thinking of leaving the Inn? That thought was intolerable, actually.

*

When John tucked his grandmother into the back seat and his parents rolled down the windows to thank me for a lovely evening, both John and I waved goodbye as they drove through the gate. Darlene and her husband hugged us as well, and Karen had disappeared minutes ago. Colette and Mark were in the kitchen drying Colette's plates to take home.

"Thanks for the great party. It was nice of you and Colette to put it together," John said to me after his folks had left.

"You're welcome," I said. "Do you mind if I say something?"

"Not at all," John said, and he stood facing me. He looked handsome that night—beaming almost—probably because he had been surrounded by so much love and affection. I tried to find the words, but they wouldn't come out as I stood there, fighting to say the right thing and not the wrong thing, but not actually knowing what the right thing to say was. I couldn't admit to eavesdropping…

"Go ahead," he said, "I'm listening."

"I know. I just don't know how to say it…what to say…"

"Just say what's on your mind."

I looked at him standing there and wondered if his heart felt as if it could leap out of his chest the same way mine felt at that moment.

"I think I've been somewhat dishonest, and I don't want to do that to you."

He held up his hand as if to motion "stop," and I immediately stopped talking, as I was taken aback by his gesture.

"You know what, Milly? I don't mean to cut you off or be rude, but I don't think I want to have this conversation right now. It's my birthday. I enjoyed the kayak today, and tonight…you and Colette went to great lengths to put this dinner together, my family had a great time, my grandmother adores you, and I don't want either of us to say anything that might taint this day. Let's just say goodnight for now, okay?"

He caught me off guard and left me so dumbfounded and speechless that my heart was racing faster than it had before. I stood there with my mouth open. My apparent shock and his unwillingness to communicate at that moment, however, didn't prevent him from bending down to kiss me on my cheek, and then he strode off in the direction of his cottage.

He meant what he said, and he did not look back.

*

I returned to the kitchen, a little astounded, and I tried to keep it together. My hands were shaking, but I wanted to help Colette and Mark, and we put everything she brought with her back into her car. It was eleven-thirty by then, and I told Colette to take the morning off, and that I would handle the breakfast.

"No," she said. "That's my job."

"Not on your day off it's not."

"I feel awful taking you up on that offer."

"Don't. I'll get up and do it tomorrow. You and Mark enjoy a morning together for once."

Mark squeezed Colette's shoulder, and she walked over to me and gave me a hug.

"I think he was touched," she said, referring to John.

"Yes, but something's going on. Do you know what?"

Mark could see that we were about to have a quick conversation, so he politely said goodnight and told Colette he would meet her at the car.

"I do, I think. Do you want to know?"

"Yes," I said. "He just told me he didn't want to talk to me and walked away."

"He loves you."

The words hung in the air, and I didn't know how to react. How do you respond to something like that when you cannot even imagine yourself loveable? Until three month ago, I was a disastrous mess who wallowed in self-pity and sadness, somewhere between mourning and feeling guilty. How in the world could John love me?

"He doesn't know me well enough to love me," I said.

"He knows you well enough that he didn't like knowing you went out with Miles Channing last night."

I folded my arms and looked at Colette in disbelief, waiting for her to finish.

"If you want my opinion, he's loved you since he first met you. Since you used to come here and visit your parents when you were grieving. He's loved you—everything about you—for a long time. Why do you think he's hung around here for so long? Before your parents told us you were going to take over, he was contemplating getting a master's degree and moving south. Then, he heard you were coming, and he stayed. For you. To help you."

What she was saying could not be true. All of it could not be true. Why? And how could he have loved me then? I was not to be loved then. I was only thinking of Gil then.

Gil. I missed Gil. How the hell was I standing in this kitchen having this conversation trying to navigate through life without him? It was still surreal. It made me wonder what the pain must be like for people who were lucky enough to spend thirty, forty, or fifty years together and then lose their spouse. No wonder you hear about longtime spouses dying one right after the other. Sometimes loss like that was insurmountable.

I told Colette I had to go—I couldn't think about any of it now.

She must have seen the stunned look on my face because she apologized to me and said she shouldn't have said anything at all.

I left the kitchen and went back to my cottage, closed the door behind me, and paced back and forth. I checked the time on the clock; it was four-thirty in the morning in Ireland, which was much too early to call my parents. It was also too late to call my sister. She would be sound asleep.

There I was again, alone in the stillness and irksome quiet of the cottage. I went to my refrigerator and poured myself another glass of wine.

I was living in the damn moment, and this was where it got me.

*

I scanned Nana's journal looking for something to help me, something relatable, one of her sage thoughts that might...

And then I saw it.

24 December 1935

It's Christmas Eve, and I'm alone. It's been over two years since Ferio's death, and here I am with a barely decorated Christmas tree and no presents underneath it. My shoes are ragged and I ate another bowl of leftover soup. I'm going to visit my family next week, but I had to stay in Oxford today for my customers' last minute dress fittings and alterations and church services. I will spend the day alone tomorrow, or perhaps go to Gertie's house for supper.

What no one ever speaks of with regard to being a widow is that the days are endless. The nights are long and hauntingly quiet. Sometimes I pace at night or think I hear noises outside my windows. It's not always pleasant to be alone.

My friends say there is a man they would like for me to meet. He is slight-ly younger than I am, but he owns some land and a small farm. Honestly, I'm not looking for anything new. I don't even know how I would adjust to something like that when I'm still missing what I had.

They tell me to give it a chance, to not be small-minded. They say he is a kind and decent man who will help me forget the loneliness and offer companionship. I told them I would think about it.

For now, I don't mind being alone with my thoughts, except when the wind rattles the house, and somehow I still sense Ferio is with me in some way. I don't know if this is true or just what I want to believe, but until I no longer feel it, I'm not exactly sure how to persevere.

I stopped reading there for a moment because I did not feel

the same way. I've never had the feeling that Gil was still with me, watching over me. I've always felt that he is gone, perhaps in Heaven, but certainly not here in a spiritual way. I have his memories, of course, but I've never had the sense that he is still a presence. The day he died, he was gone, and the only thing I've clung to are the reruns of us together that I play over and over again in my head to remind myself that he lived. Nana and I were different with regard to those emotions and that sixth sense. I never felt that. Not ever.

I continued to read on, taking note of the dates, when I landed on this:

9 May 1936

After many months, I agreed to go on a picnic lunch with the gentleman my friends wanted me to meet. Edward is medium height, somewhat lanky, though strong, with a chiseled face and deep-set eyes that are filled with kindness. He is easy to talk to which surprised me. We even laughed a couple of times while we were together. He is gentle and thoughtful and brought me an abundance of roses from his garden. He held my hand.

When the afternoon was over and he walked me home, I didn't want him to leave.

For a moment, I felt incredibly guilty about it, but I told myself it was okay. No more perpetual sadness, I said to myself.

I didn't want Edward to leave, and I told him so.

I turned to read the next entry, and there wasn't one. I skimmed the last several pages of the journal, and the pages were blank. That was it. That was the last entry. No other parting words, no other sentiments about Ferio and moving on from the depths of the loss of her soulmate and husband. Just that singular, final entry. Edward, my dear, sweet grandfather, had come into her life on a spring day, and my grandmother stopped writing in this journal and apparently hid it away—the journal that contained stories of Ferio and all that was before Edward. In essence, she just locked it up and threw away the key. The memories of Ferio were buried in the basement in a box and she never told my mother—her only child—about the man she loved so dearly prior to loving Edward. She may have kept him alive in her heart, but we'll honestly never know why she chose never to discuss him with any of us.

It was curious, the choices we made in life.

Once Nana died, who was left to remember Ferio? When people died, their only hope of a legacy was left in the hands of those who outlived them and who could actually tell their stories. Now, Ferio, Nana and Grandpa were all gone, and we, those who knew them or knew of them, were the only ones who remained to tell the tales of their lives, their loves, their hopes, and their dreams. The same was true with Gil. It should always be the responsibility of the living to keep our family histories alive.

Miles was right. We owed it to ourselves to tell the stories that we knew.

Maybe it was my turn to tell mine.

CHAPTER 18

October was my favorite month of the year. The humidity faded and we were left with spectacular weather. A few days of rain in late September were a small sacrifice to pay for glorious sunshine for the month that followed. The weeping willow blew softly in the breeze as I straightened up the outdoor furniture, and I stood by the water and inhaled the scent of autumn that would soon arrive as the sun rose behind me.

After John's birthday celebration, I focused on my work. There was no need to discuss anything with him, as he clearly let me know that he was not open to talking. Colette and I moved past our differing opinions and engaged in small talk in the kitchen in the mornings. John and I kept our conversations short and sweet, mostly about procedures or Inn upkeep. He also chose to spend a lot of his free time on Plane To Sea or in the kayak. There was a lot to be done at the Inn, especially with regard to cleaning it and maintaining it after a long, hot summer. To add to the busy nature, Karen had returned to college to complete her senior year, and her absence left little time for a social life, which kept me distracted with the Inn more than ever.

Miles and I corresponded several times through email and text messaging because I actually needed his advice. When I told him I was starting to write again, he sounded so pleased with him-self, as if he coached someone back to the writing life, back from the dead.

"Any chance you will be visiting soon?" I texted.

"Not as of now, but I will keep you posted," he texted back.

My parents checked on me several times, more than usual, and I became suspicious that Colette may have said something to my mother. Regardless, I was in a complete funk, and I feared I was closing myself off from people, a habit that had become my standard mode of operation.

The kayak appeared, and I could hear the swishing of the paddles meeting the water. John had abandoned his morning run in lieu of a kayak workout. He saw me standing at the water's edge and waved, and I waved back to him.

I thought about the paintings in his room, about how I chose to shut out the world, about the night we spent together in my cot-tage, and about how he forged on despite his horrible, haunting memories. Seeing him out on that kayak, alone, that morning—I can't tell you how it affected me. But I can tell you this: that solitary moment on the lawn of the Inn made me cognizant of the amount of time I'd spent grieving and in pain, and that maybe it was time for me to attempt to move on from it; it also made me realize that I may have hurt John over the last few months. It wasn't intentional. I just hadn't been ready for something else. Yet.

However, there was a turning point for most people. My head was becoming clear, and I knew exactly what I had to do.

*

John came through the office door freshly showered and ready for the day. I was organizing the bills, sitting behind the desk, and I watched him move to his station. "Good morning," he said, cheerfully.

"Good morning," I said. "How was the kayak this morning?"

"Great. Did you see how smooth the river was? Like glass. I love it like that."

He began to rummage through the bookings for the day, a cup of coffee in his hand. I was watching him out of the corner of my eye, waiting for the right moment. He paused, and looked up.

"Did you take this reservation for the Dumas couple?"

"Yes," I said.

"They are coming today?"

"Yes," I said. "Darlene is already cleaning that room."

"Great," he said. "I remember them from last year. He's an elderly gentleman, so I'll make sure I'm around to get their bags to their room."

"That would be great," I said.

He turned on the local radio station and lowered the volume, in order to not disturb me. John liked having background noise in the office, whereas the quiet never bothered me. I'd become quite used to silence and didn't much care for morning deejays who talked too much and didn't play enough music.

"I was wondering if you had any interest in going to the St. Michaels Art Show with me in a couple of weeks," I said. It took everything in me to utter the words, but I felt courageous, and put it out there.

He looked up from his paperwork and across the room at me. "Sure," he said, "but who will cover?"

"I already have that arranged," I said. "I touched base with Karen, and she is coming home that weekend for her mother's birthday, and she said she could work the desk for a few hours."

"Ok, then. That sounds like a plan," he said nonchalantly.

"And when are we going to make some more muffins? It feels as if it's been a while."

"Since when did you become enthusiastic about baking in the kitchen?"

"Since now," I said.

*

When John left to go collect the remainder of our tomatoes from the garden for Colette and I had a few moments of privacy, I dialed the phone. My mother answered immediately on the first ring.

"That's so weird—I was just about to dial you!" she exclaimed.

"How's it going with the Inn and everything with Devon?" I asked.

"Oh, great. It seems to be going well so far. He had his first guests last weekend, and we're helping him get organized."

"Do you think you're going to stay the whole year? Or will you be coming back sooner?"

There was a pregnant pause, and I could hear some sort of commotion in the background.

"You want to know when we're coming home?"

"Yes," I said. "I was just wondering if you had a handle on that."

"We haven't set a date yet, sweetheart, but you know that we'll come home whenever you want us to if things aren't going well there."

"It's not that," I said, twirling my hair. "It's just—"

"What is it?"

"It's John," I said. "A few weeks ago Colette made a comment that he might have feelings for me. Did he ever say anything to you?"

Another pause. "He's always been fond of you." That response. So telling. She knew. She knew something and wasn't sharing it with me.

"Did you set this whole overseas thing up so John and I could spend time together? Did you conveniently leave for Ireland so I could conveniently live next door to John?"

"Well...I..."

"Good grief, Mom."

"Well, didn't you tell me Nana's friends set her up with Grandpa?"

"Yes, but you didn't know that when you hatched this plan."

"But we had your best interest at heart just as Nana's friends had hers at heart."

"I'll talk to you later," I said.

"Love you," she said.

CHAPTER 19

We were scheduled to go to St. Michaels in the afternoon, and Karen arrived at the Inn to help manage the place in our absence. John was upbeat and ready to go early, and I came running out of the cottage right on time.

"Thanks so much for filling in, Karen," I told her. "What time are you celebrating your mom's birthday?"

"Tonight around seven. My whole family is coming over for dinner."

"We won't make you late, I promise. We should be gone three hours and then we'll be back."

"Enjoy yourselves," she said, and she gave a little nod to John that I probably wasn't supposed to see.

St. Michaels, located about twenty minutes away, was picturesque, historic, and absolutely charming. It was alive with visitors and shoppers, and as we made our way toward the heart of the town, we could see it was bustling—more so than in quiet Oxford. I was just excited to be away for a few hours. I was also slightly nervous. After all, I had asked John to come with me, and whether he considered it a date or not was yet to be discovered.

We were fortunate and found a parking space right on the street; someone was pulling out just as we approached and we snagged the spot. There were soft fluffy clouds in the clear, blue sky, and it had become cooler overnight. I wore a blouse, cardigan, and jeans tucked into tall boots, and John was in jeans and a long-sleeved black t-shirt. We walked side by side to the area where the white tents displayed artwork of all kinds.

"So, you enjoy looking at art?" he asked.

"Sometimes," I said. "You?"

"Very much." I didn't pursue anything further. If he wanted to tell me more, he would.

We wandered in and out of the exhibits looking at paintings that ran the gamut from waterscapes to portraits. I actually knew very little about art, except for what I learned in my college fine arts class called Art Appreciation that we, the students, lovingly nick-named "Art in the Dark." The course required us to view slides of famous works of art on a large projector screen in a lecture hall with the lights off while the professor offered the history of the pieces and the artists. I could identify impressionist and fauvist style paintings because they were my favorites. Artists such as Monet, Renoir, and Matisse were easy for me to pinpoint, but others were more challenging. John pointed to a painting of the St. Michaels harbor at night and called it photorealism, because the painting was so incredibly lifelike and mimicked reality.

He stood and studied a watercolor of the Ocean City boardwalk, paying careful attention to it. I studied him.

"I know this artist," he finally said. "I grew up with him. I think he lives in a big home in Bethany Beach now."

"Well, it's very beautiful," I replied, remarking on the painting.

"I have to give these people credit. It takes a lot of guts to show your work to the world and sit back and wait for criticism. I give you the same credit, as well. It must be tough to write something and then publish it because you know some people will love it, some will hate it, and some will just think it's okay."

"Very true," I said. "Whenever you do anything creative you have to have thick skin. I became used to the criticism, but, I can assure you, the positive feedback always outweighs the negative."

"I don't know if that philosophy held true for the movie *Waterworld* with Kevin Costner."

I laughed. "Okay, there are always exceptions to the rules."

We moved on to look at the next piece, and I wondered if he would tell me about his artistic talents. When he didn't mention anything, I was disappointed. After we finished wandering the tents and talking about the various pieces that were displayed, I suggested we get a bite to eat and a drink at Foxy's on the water. It was right in the middle of the day, and there were plenty of tables available.

John ordered the grilled mahi-mahi burger, and I opted for the fish tacos. A musician played acoustic guitar on the deck, the sound of the breeze catching his microphone every once in a while, causing it to make a "whooshing" sound. Around us, people relaxed at tables and ate along the water.

"I love eating outside," I said. "I'm not looking forward to being cooped up when it gets colder. How quiet is the Inn during the winter months?"

"You'd be surprised," he said. "It's actually not as quiet as you would think. January and February are probably the slowest months, but there's rarely a night when someone isn't staying there."

"That's good to know. I always wondered how my parents fared during those colder months."

"Your mother does a good job of hosting activities at the Inn in the winter months—did she tell you about them?"

"Some," I said. "I've got her list in the office somewhere. Which begs the question: how do you cope in the winter months, mister I-run-outside-and-kayak-daily guy?"

"Pretty well," he said. "There's more free time, so I spend it doing some of my hobbies."

"Like exercising indoors?"

"Yes," he said, "among other things."

"Such as? Care to tell?" I asked, raising my eyebrows.

"Maybe, but not now. When I'm ready, I might show you instead."

"I'm intrigued," I said with a smile.

Just then, we noticed two people stepping onto the dock from their large sailboat. It took us a second to realize it was Greg and Mona who were waving at us, trying to get our attention.

"Oh, hi!" I said when I saw them approaching. They had docked their boat and were wearing their boaters' preppy attire. Mona was dressed in white tailored pants and a stripped sweater with a scarf around her neck and big sunglasses; Greg wore madras shorts, a blue long-sleeved t-shirt, and boat shoes. They looked as if they just modeled for a sailing magazine.

"Mind if we join you guys?" Mona asked, after hugging and kissing us.

"We would love it," John said, looking for confirmation from me.

"Of course," I said. "Please do."

Our food had not yet arrived, so the server took their orders. When Greg ordered a beer, I asked Mona if she wanted to join me and have a glass of white wine. She declined, and asked for water with lemon.

"I'm so glad we ran into you both here," Mona said. "We have some exciting news to share." She smiled at Greg, and the two of them were beaming. Seeing them so full of happiness, John and I looked at each other, and I think we both guessed what she was going to say.

"We're expecting!" she said. "And if you're adding it up in your heads, yes, I was a few weeks pregnant when we were married. My dress was a little snug, but we had already set the date, so…what the heck, right? We're feeling pretty modern. Make the baby before we say 'I do' and all that."

"Well, I'm really happy for you both," I said. "Congratulations!"

"Me, too," John said. We made a toast and clinked our glasses.

When our food arrived and we began to eat, I was thankful for the bit of reprieve from talking. While I was tremendously excited for Mona and Greg, the news of her pregnancy brought back memories of my own miscarriage. I'd wanted to have a family so badly. Still, I managed a smile. Nevertheless, instead of dwelling on what might have been, I decided I would finish the baby blanket I started way back when and give it to them as a gift. It was so close to completion. From somewhere deep inside I knew that things don't always turn out the way we want them to, but the reality is no one can change fate. What is meant to be is meant to be. Questioning it doesn't do any good.

"So, how do you like running the Inn?" Mona said, tearing me from my internal thoughts. "Do you miss Washington?"

"So far, I'm really loving my time here," I said. "I don't miss Washington at all. It's a far cry from being a writer, which was my former job, but hospitality is growing on me, I suppose. It was my mother's idea for me do this."

"John told me. He told me what happened to your husband. I was so sorry to hear," Mona said. "Sometimes life deals us a strange hand."

"Yes, it does," I said, and took a sip of my wine. "But, let us not think unhappy thoughts right now when you and Greg are sharing such wonderful news."

"Thank you," Mona said. "But please know that although we don't know each other that well yet, I'm looking forward to spending more time with you and getting to know you. I have no doubt we will be great friends. And I'm available for a night out—without the boys—anytime you want."

"Good to know," I said. "Because I really love a good chick flick now and then."

"I'm in," she replied. "And Greg hates them. Also, if you organize any of those wine tasting things like your mother set up last winter, I'll be there, too. Of course, I won't be able to drink because of the baby, but I can help with anything you need."

*

In an attempt not to be late to relieve Karen so that she could make it to her mother's party, we paid our bill and said goodbye to our friends as they got back on their boat to sail it back home to their dock. We promised to get together with them soon, and they invited us over for dessert one night in order to use the Crate & Barrel fondue set they got as a wedding gift from Mona's sister.

"I'm sorry our lunch became a foursome. Thanks for being so great with Greg and Mona. I know they have good intentions even though they can be a little overwhelming at times," John said as we rode back to the Inn.

"No worries. They're just two happy, bubbly people. Honestly, I wish I could be more like them. You know—agonize less, enjoy life more, live in the moment."

"Me too," he said.

We listened to the hum of the car, and then John turned on the radio in an attempt to mask the silence, trying to find something appropriate to play. When he came up empty handed after clicking all the dials, he pushed the CD button and James Taylor's smooth voice filled in where words between us were lacking.

I should have known he liked James Taylor. You learn something about people by the choices they make with regard to music. With his soft, soothing voice and clearly enunciated lyrics, we let JT take us the rest of the way home without uttering another word.

*

"I hope you don't think this is too forward," John said after we sent Karen on her way, "but I was wondering if you would like to come over for a little bit. There's something I want to show you."

"Sure," I said. "Sounds nice."

We walked up the steps to his place, and I reminded myself that I couldn't let on that I had been inside when I searched for the kayak information without his knowledge. I wanted to confess it, but I didn't dare. Plus, I felt it would be inappropriate to tell John I had snooped and seen his artistic talent. For the time being, I chose to keep my mouth shut.

He opened the door and we stepped inside. I immediately remembered the scent of the place—it smelled like him: warm, musky, inviting, and undoubtedly masculine, a far cry from my own very feminine set up next door. He flicked on the light in the main living area, and he walked me over to his desk.

"I don't just show anyone these, you know," he said, smirking at me. "And you don't have to say you like everything, but I would be interested to see which ones you like best."

He uncovered them, and there were all the paintings, sketches, and drawings. "So, the cat's out of the bag now," he said. "In my free time, I do this."

I looked at him, and because we had such a lovely day, I decided to come clean. Why would I want to hide from him that I had an inclination?

"I have a confession to make," I said. "I kind of knew you were an artist."

"How?"

"When we were trying to get the model number of the kayak you wanted, I sort of snuck in here while you were running. I just happened to see the artwork on your desk."

"Is that why you invited me to the art show today?"

"I thought you might like it."

I wasn't sure if this information would make him angry, but I didn't want to lie. There was something in his manner that made me think he might actually have appreciated that I was forthcoming with that information. We'd been pretty honest with each other since we'd met, and it would have kept a barrier between us and I didn't want that.

"Well, I guess I'm flattered that you were thoughtful that way. Thank you."

"You're welcome," I said. "And I'm sorry I had to trespass, but I'm glad we pulled off the gift. Now, can you show me your work?"

We spent the next hour combing through some of John's pieces. There were so many, he was selective about the ones for which he wanted my feedback. Of the three, the painting that moved me the most was of a soldier who had died—the one he knew who succumbed to the IED. It was a hauntingly realistic portrait of a man, and the eyes held such sadness in the depiction. There were two other paintings that caught my eye. The first was a beach scene with lightning dancing across the sky; somehow John was able to make the scene so realistic, beautiful, and petrifying all at the same time. The second was a rendition of his grandmother's house, the one she owned until she moved into the senior home. It was full of character, with abundant gardens full of vibrant colors with pops of pinks and purples and yellows mixed in with the lush greens in the garden. The tone of it looked as if it should be a postcard or a poster, it was just so compelling.

"I'm giving this one to my grandmother for Christmas. She lived in the house forever. I've hesitated to give it to her because I don't want to make her cry."

"If that happens, she will cry tears of joy," I said. "It's stunning."

He offered me a glass of wine, and I accepted. We sat there talking until we noticed the time. It was late, and our day together had been so lovely and comfortable and honest, I hated for it to end, but I was yawning, and my yawning was making him yawn.

"I'd better get some sleep," I said, not wanting to overstay my welcome. We had covered a lot of ground, especially because he had willingly shared his paintings and incredible talent with me. "You really should do something with this incredible gift of yours. Your work should have been displayed in those tents today."

"Thank you for saying so. Maybe some day. Still trying to work up the nerve. I equate it to sharing poetry—not everyone has the ability to share easily. That's something I need to work on," he said.

"Let me know if I can help," I said. I walked closer to him and leaned up and kissed him on the cheek. "Thanks for a great afternoon—and evening," I said. "See you in the morning?"

"See you then," he said, and he opened the door and watched me walk the short distance to my cottage. I waved when I opened the door, and he waved back.

*

I found myself still awake at two in the morning wrestling with my own thoughts and doing my best not to allow any guilt to creep into my assessment of the day. Recently, I found comfort asking myself, "What would Nana do?" in certain situations. Of course, my late grandmother couldn't respond, but I could swear I felt something in the air, or perhaps it was my own wishful thinking that she might be able to communicate with me through signs or small epiphanies. The lingering voice I heard in my head from immersing myself in the writings and breathings of her journal was clearly hers; I could imagine the lull of her voice, the inflection rising from her words, the sweetness of her observations. Now that I was done reading and her thoughts were done, I was left with a voice. There was nothing more for me to read after Ferio died and she met my grandfather, however, I cherished the insights I gained from her about life after a tragedy. Maybe there really was such as thing as a fairy godmother—or grandmother—in my case.

Today might have been the first time I felt contentment with another person for an extended amount of time. John's demeanor and gentlemanly behavior always made me feel comfortable; he understood me. There was something chivalrous and sweet about his ability to let me be and not push me into anything that didn't feel right.

After saying a quick prayer, my eyelids became heavy, and I felt thankful for my mother's crazy idea to involve me here at the Inn for the year. What an unusual turn of events. I was enjoying a quiet, simple life among sweet, loving people. It was undoubtedly a sublime place to be reflective and become restored.

As I stretched on the bed and rolled onto my back, my head resting on the pillow and the covers pulled up to my neck, I became still and put my hand on my chest. In the quiet of the cottage, I listened to my heartbeat: it was beating steady and strong, and it was undeniably alive.

CHAPTER 20

The next morning, John and I were sitting at our desks in the office attempting to plow through paperwork and make a list of repairs that needed attention. Additionally, I decided to organize a wine tasting in November, just as my mother had done for the last five years. I was reading through her notes, and asking John questions when two new guests arrived for check-in.

John stood and welcomed them, began to process the payment for the two nights they would be with us, and handed over a key to their suite. I smiled at them when John introduced me and wished them a lovely time at the Inn, reminding them to join us for afternoon tea at four o'clock if they would be around.

"Mrs. Foster?" the woman said, looking at me, her eyebrows raised. Strangely, her voice sounded familiar.

"Milly," I said. "You can call me Milly."

"Yes, I know," she said. "Mrs. Milly Foster?"

"Yes," I said, quizzically looking at her.

"I'm glad to see you looking so well. I'm Officer Jones—Felicia Jones—"

Once she spoke those words in that distinct voice of hers, I knew. She was the officer from—the one who had to tell me about Gil. I saw her that night. I remembered opening my eyes to look at her, seeing the sheer kindness she exuded while she took care of me, called the paramedics and my mother, placed me on the couch, and had her partner take the roast out of the oven. It was she who was there with me that night.

I stood and walked over to her. I reached out to hug her. "Thank you, Officer Jones. Thank you for your kindness."

"Call me Felicia," she whispered.

I wasn't sure if John understood the connection, but I could see he was touched by the display that unfolded. Officer Jones's husband appeared to be very proud of his wife as he stood back and let us connect.

"Welcome," I said, letting go of her and squeezing her hands as I addressed them both. "Welcome to Inn Significant. It's so good to see you. We sincerely hope you will enjoy your stay here with us."

*

"Old friend of yours?" John asked later as we picked a couple of last items from the food garden, including three pumpkins that had grown quite large. We were dressed to get dirty in what had been a flourishing garden—to clean, rake, and prepare it for next season. The garden was cluttered with dying and dead plants, crusty vines, and limp stalks, and our garden gloves were filthy with dirt.

"She was the one who had to tell me Gil died," I said. "Brave lady."

"It's not an easy job in any regard, is it?" John said. I thought the same was true for military personnel who have to announce bad news to families of lost loved ones. What an unenviable task some people have as jobs. I wondered if John ever had to relay that kind of news to someone, but I didn't want to ask him at that moment.

We placed the pumpkins in the wheelbarrow along with the remaining basil and oregano that had remarkably stayed quite hearty and we raked the garden, putting it back to its original state, back to how it looked before the food garden became lush and picturesque and edible. We both felt a sense of accomplishment.

"You did well, John. I would say this garden was a big success," I said.

"And pretty delicious, too, thanks to Colette," he added.

"After we clean up, would you mind taking a look at something I've written?" I asked, having finally found the courage to ask him. It was something I finished a couple of weeks ago, but I had taken some time to work on it—to perfect it.

"Of course," he said, "however, I should be honest—writing is definitely not my forte. But I do consider myself a good reader."

"That's all I need," I said.

*

When the last dish was put away from the afternoon tea in the parlor and the sun began to set, John and I walked to the office. I fiddled with my laptop, found the document, and hit print.

"Okay, so you showed me your remarkable art masterpieces. I certainly won't call this a masterpiece by any stretch of the imagination, but it's my first blog post from the Inn. It took me all summer to figure out how I wanted to write and position this, and here it is. Feedback of any kind is welcome, good or bad. Promise?"

"You have my word," he said.

He picked up the freshly printed pages, and held them in his hands. His eyes moved across the page, as he became comfortable in his chair. I tried not to stare at him as he read, but it was difficult not to. You can sometimes interpret what a person thinks simply from the nonverbal communication they offer, and whether it was positive or negative, that was left to be decided. I studied him, gauging what little I could, because his expression remained steady and thoughtful throughout.

Inn Significant: The Blog

Welcome.
It's October now, and I've finally written the first blog post from Inn Significant. My parents own this incredible property here in Oxford, Mary-

land, a gem of a small town with hidden treasures everywhere. However, my mother and father are on an adventure in Ireland for a year, and they've left me, their eldest daughter, in charge of this place in their absence. My mother is a crafty woman who knows her daughter better than anyone. I'm thankful for her love and affection and for trusting me with this marvelous property. I hope I do you proud, Mom and Dad. And to my sister, thank you for helping to revamp the website. We're all happy with its new look.

I came to the Inn on a weeknight in May. There was a big banner over the door welcoming me. Not to be maudlin, but my husband had died two years prior, and I hadn't quite been the same since then. His loss was catastrophic for me; I wasn't sure how to move on. That was, until my mother got involved.

Having quit my job as a writer for a magazine and pretty much wallowing in my own sorrow, I was persuaded to come here, although I was probably still half out of my wits, and run the place. I received a crash course in hospitality, and without my trusty associates—John, Colette, Darlene, and Karen—I'm not sure I could have pulled it off. But here I am.

And I've embraced and cherished every moment of it.

This place has a special power—a power to heal us, whether the healing is slow and gradual, or immediately revitalizing over the course of a day or two. The energy of the river, the peacefulness of this retreat, the sweetness of the people, the serenity of the Inn, and the open arms of Oxford have all played a part in the return to the person I used to be.

And that's the truth: with each passing day, I'm finding my way back to happiness and love.

Though none of us who has ever lost someone dear will ever quite be the same, we must continue to carry on—for them, for us, for those who love us. My parents gave me a gift when they asked me to come here; they allowed me to reconnect with dreams, aspirations, and love.

Miraculously, I have hope again.

When John, the kindest, most trustworthy, giving person I know and rely on daily at the Inn, found an old journal in the basement of the main house and placed it in my hands, I sensed something unique and meaningful was about to happen. In the 1930s, my own grandmother had loved and lost her first husband, a man named Ferio—a man none of us ever knew existed. In her journal, I read how she and Ferio navigated the harrowing years of the depression. My grandmother never told her own family—her own daughter—that she had been married prior to marrying my grandfather, Edward, my mother's father and the man she married several years after Ferio's death. Although my grandmother and grandfather have been dead for over ten years and had a long life together, I began to feel a strong bond with my grandmother through her heartfelt writing and storytelling that was carefully documented in her journal; I felt even more connected to her than I did when she was alive because we shared similar fates. She and I had both lost our husbands at young ages; we both thought we would spend the rest of our lives with our respective husbands; and both of our husbands died tragically from the result of accidents.

Reading the written words of my grandmother in her journal helped me understand that we are not alone in anything we go through. Others have gone through similar circumstances. And they've found love again. Sometimes it's even right underneath our noses.

After living as an unredeemed basket case for years, my life is finally taking a turn for the better. Inn Significant was formerly my grandparents' home and has been in our family for over seventy years. It has evolved into a place where people gather, exchange stories, and find comfort in the serene surroundings and welcoming camaraderie. Every guest I meet has a unique story and a reason for visiting, whether it is just to escape the hectic world for a day or two, sit and read in an Adirondack chair or hammock by the river, commune with nature by enjoying activities outdoors, or enjoy sightseeing while on the Eastern Shore.

Like me, no matter who you are or where you call home, I hope you will find a connection to the Inn—a respite from the busy world—and perhaps think of it as your home away from home and a place that truly is significant.

~Milly Foster, October 2012

He cleared his throat and looked up at me. I'd seen a similar expression on Gil's face years ago when he read a meaningful card I had written for our anniversary.

"This is really beautiful," he said.

"You think?"

"I know. And I'll be interested to see what else will come from that big heart of yours."

He was smiling at me, his eyes glistening. Without saying another word, I walked closer to him. There was something in his demeanor that instant that made me so sure of what it was I was about to do: it was the way he took the time to read what I'd written, that he was moved by the words in a way that only he and I might understand, connect with, and know are true, and then, and perhaps most importantly, by the way he looked at me.

"So, it's okay? It doesn't need any tweaking."

"To me, it's perfect just as it is."

He turned the leather, swivel chair to face me. I reached over and touched his face and looked at him. I cleared my mind of all thoughts that could prevent me from doing what I wanted to do. I was living in the moment, freeing myself. This was about the here and now, not what was or what could have been. I bent down so that my lips could meet his, and I kissed him. It was meant to happen right there, at that time, when both of us were fully aware of what we were doing and that it was the step toward something meaningful. His mouth was warm and sweet and full of longing. I wrapped my arms, body, and soul around him, not wanting to let him go, and he did the same; I breathed in all that he is. We found each other there, in that chair, as we became tangled up in something bigger than either of us wanted to control or ignore any longer.

For the first time in almost three years, I allowed someone to touch me, stroke my hair, and passionately kiss me, and I responded in kind. I granted myself permission to tumble into the moment, stop fighting the past, and just fall.

My heart was pounding. I looked deeply into his eyes, held his gaze, and smiled. I felt alive again.

*

"Wait here," John said, as we exited the office an hour later, straightening out our clothing and fixing our hair.

"You mean right here?"

"Yes. Don't move."

I watched him jog across the lawn to his cottage and disappear inside. I kept my feet just as they were there, firmly planted. The air was sweet and flowed through me as dusk descended upon the town. It had become cool, and I pulled my sweater around me tightly. Within minutes, John, smiling broadly with a glint of mystery in his eyes, returned with a cooler in his hand and a big, wool blanket folded across his arm.

"I forwarded the main line to my cell," he said. "Let's go."

"Where?"

"To Plane To Sea, of course," he said with a wink.

I looped my arm through John's, and we walked along Strand to the marina.

"I don't know what it is about this place," I said. "There's something magical about it. It grounds you."

"I think for people like us who have experienced traumatic events, it helps remind us that a place can certainly heal wounds, but it's the people you meet in the place that have the power to bring you back."

He was a sensitive, gentle, and compassionate person. I knew that now more than ever; we shared so many of the same bruises as well as the same hopes and dreams. I rested my head on his shoulder and we walked the rest of the way listening to the water hit the shore, the swirl of the breeze, and the sound of our own feet as we approached the marina.

John stepped aboard first, and then reached for my hand to guide me aboard. I felt an immediate spark as my hand touched the warmth of his skin and felt his grip on me, and my singular desire was to be as physically close to him as possible. He opened a bottle of wine, poured it into the two stemmed glasses he packed, and set up a little table to place the cheese, crackers, and grapes he brought as our snack. The moon was just beginning to brighten in the night sky, and he put his arm around me as I moved next to him, cuddled under the moonlight in each other's arms. The waves gently rocked the boat and the hardships and suffering we had endured separately seemed to float away with the tide.

CHAPTER 21

I was up bright and early and left John sleeping in my cottage, tucked beneath the freshly laundered white sheets and down comforter. We talked all night, and somewhere around four in the morning, he fell asleep. My adrenaline was running so high that sleep was impossible—and unwelcome. Butterflies flitted in my stomach. How could I sleep when life had opened my eyes to new possibilities? To the idea of happiness? To possible love? To letting go of guilt? I quietly said a prayer, and then, speaking only to her I uttered, "Thank you, Nana," in a whisper.

I dressed and made my way to the main house. Colette and I prepared the breakfast the next morning together. Despite the lack of rest, I was perky and upbeat as I placed the morning's meal for the guests on the huntboard in the dining room. I selected a Tony Bennett disc for the morning's diners, and raised the volume slightly.

"You're extraordinarily cheery this morning," Colette said, commenting on my blissful disposition.

"I am. I'm feeling alive this morning, Colette. What a great morning to be up with the sun and see the gulls flying around on the river. The leaves are changing and the blue sky this morning is absolutely stunning. Did you see how perfect it is outside? I'm so lucky to be here. Remind me to thank my parents, will you?"

Colette stopped what she was doing and placed her hands on her hips. She smiled, and I knew she knew simply by deduction: John was not here, I was, and I couldn't shut up. All was right with my world.

"Well, it's about time," she said.

Felicia Jones and her husband entered the room, and Colette and I offered them juice and coffee.

"This place seems to agree with you, Mrs. Foster, and I can see why." I looked at her and she quickly corrected herself. "I mean, Milly."

"Thanks, Felicia. I do love it here. I think I may be rediscovering myself. Nevertheless, I can't tell you how happy I am that you both stayed with us. I hope you found it relaxing and special. I hope you were able to unwind. I can only imagine how hectic and stressful your job must be. I have nothing but the utmost respect for you." I gave her a big hug.

Her husband spoke on behalf of both of them. "You have no idea. Felicia needed it—we both did. I think it's the most relaxed we've been in years. This place might have some magic in its back pocket."

"I think you may be right," I said, smiling and shaking my head. "You're echoing the same exact sentiment I just said to someone last night."

*

As Colette and I cleaned up the morning's dishes, John entered the kitchen looking handsome—and happy. He wore blue jeans and a button down. As he drew closer to me, I could smell his cologne, and it ignited a desire that still lingered from the previous night's intimacy and bonding. I saw him look at Colette out of the corner of my eyes, and I mouthed, "She knows." He smiled, and then came over to kiss me on the lips. Colette witnessed the tail end of our embrace and open display of affection, became a little embarrassed, and blushed.

"Oh, jeez. Get a room, you two," she said, waving her dishtowel.

"Something tells me that can be arranged," John said, and we all laughed, but not before Collette walked over and whacked him on the backside with the spatula she was drying.

"Oh, Lord-y," she exclaimed. "What have I gotten myself into?"

It was so funny to see her flustered. How could we not have a little fun with it? It was a light, silly moment, and because I was punchy from lack of sleep, it was even funnier to me, and I laughed until I cried.

*

"You look tired. Are you sure you don't want to go take a little nap for a while?" John asked me later that morning, stroking my arm.

"I'm fine," I said, smiling at him. "Besides, I have to get these invitations to the post office for the wine event, and we have to decorate the Inn for the fall season. I want to get to Councell Farms before all the good stuff is taken."

"Do you want me to go pick the stuff up and you can stay here?"

"I think I'd like to go. I've got a vision brewing in my head. I cleaned out the back of the SUV so I can load it up."

I knew how I wanted to decorate the place. After researching online and printing examples and inspirational photos, I was on a mission to see this through. The wine event would be the first I would host at the Inn, and I wanted it to go well. The Inn's reputation was on the line. My mother's copious notes were helpful, and I invited all of the same folks who were on my mother's list—and a few additional ones I'd met along the way.

John walked me to the car, and I gave him a little kiss. There was a sweetness to our newfound romance, and I liked the feel of it.

"I'll see you shortly," I said.

As I drove out S. Morris Street, I noticed that a couple of

homes were up for sale. One, in particular, had always been a favorite of mine. It was a green, three-story, center hall colonial, with touches of a Victorian detail on the front porch. The third story dormer windows off the roof added personality to the place. There was even a flower box on the front, main window with vines overflowing from it. I pulled over to have a look, and found myself getting out of the car and taking a brochure from the sign that was posted on the front lawn.

This is madness, I thought. What in the world am I doing?

The home was quite affordable for me; at over three-thousand square feet, it was way more room than I needed, but it was in excellent shape. It looked as if it were kept in pristine condition. I studied the images and read the details of the home. I was intrigued. I had money sitting in the bank from the sale of my home and investments, and I knew at some point I'd actually have to buy a place and not live off the extreme kindness of my parents. My mother might go into shock at the thought of me living right down the street from her. I hadn't lived near my parents in over twenty years. Had I gone completely insane? And what would I do for a living here? How would I earn money to stay?

I brushed all those thoughts aside, because actually, the idea of how I would earn my keep seemed trivial now. After five months, the truth was, I couldn't imagine leaving. I would do whatever I could to live in Oxford. Of course, I hadn't talked to John about any of this. This notion was a complete whim, an idea so spur of the moment, that I was having trouble believing I was considering any of it. Who was this impetuous girl behind the wheel of this car?

And yet the very idea of it was making my heart do flip-flops, and I couldn't wait to return to the Inn to tell John all about it. I wanted to call my parents. I wanted to talk to Colette.

I wanted to kiss Nana's journal.

*

I returned a couple of hours later with a car stuffed with hay bales, pumpkins, gourds, string lights, and lots of mums and bacopa plants. John was waiting for me, and I was about to explode with glee at the spontaneous idea I was trying to explain. My mouth was moving so fast he had to tell me to "slow down."

"Try again, and this time feel free to breathe," he said.

"Ha, ha," I said. "Very funny. I just had the most insane epiphany. I don't know if it makes any sense or seems logical at all, but the mere thought of it is making me giddy."

"Ok...I'm listening."

"You know that green house on S. Morris on the left as you're leaving town?"

"You mean the one that's for sale?"

"You saw it?" I said. "Yes, that one."

"Yes," he said, motioning me to continue.

"I think I want to buy it."

"I think the lack of sleep has caught up to you now. I think you need to take a rest and then we can talk about it."

"But I don't want to rest. That's all I've been doing for the last three years. Now, I'm here…alive…excited. I'm living in the freaking moment, John. I want to buy that house. I want to live here. For good. Forever."

He looked at me, unsure as to what I was saying. I didn't know what I was saying, for God's sake. I could hardly control myself as crafty notions, insane ideas, and strings of untidy and ardent words flew out of my mouth at a rapid pace.

"You want to buy that house."

"I think I do."

"And what would you do here in Oxford?"

"I don't know yet. But that just seems insignificant now, doesn't it? I'll figure it out. We'll figure it out. Maybe you and I could operate a writing and art center. Or, I've been wondering, why we don't host weddings on the Inn's property? We have the room, and we could build a large barn-type structure for weddings—they're the rage now, you know—people hosting receptions in barns. Just look at Pinterest. There's probably a lot we could do besides work for Mom and Dad. Maybe we could work with Mom and Dad. Maybe I will write on the side. Maybe you'll become a personal trainer and artiste supreme. I honestly don't know. But John, for the first time in a very long time, I feel quite unlike my previous self and more like my old self, if that makes any sense at all. And much of it has to do with this spectacular place and you."

He studied me, my expressions, my gestures. He knew then that I was serious. He didn't tell me I was crazy or out of my mind. He didn't tell me I was a dreamer and that this was decided on a whim. Instead, he watched my eyes as they danced there in the late afternoon sun, full of idealistic desires and half-cocked plans. He took his hands and held my face, and looking directly into my eyes, he said with a smile, "Do you have any idea how long I've loved you?"

CHAPTER 22

The Inn looked stunning at dusk as the guests started to arrive. White lanterns lined the walkway up to the front porch, and hay bails, white pumpkins, gourds, and twinkle lights sparkled and welcomed guests. Ella Fitzgerald played softly in the background; the wine was set up on tables in the main parlor and dining areas covered in brown bags. Each wine was numbered with a specially marked, decorated tag, and guests roamed around tasting the wines and ranking them on a sheet I printed. Colette made a ridiculous amount of food, and the evening was off to a spectacular start.

Karen was home visiting with her new boyfriend, Alex, from college, and Darlene and Vic, along with Colette and Mark, were helping our guests—over fifty of them—with the wine tasting. The Inn was bustling and merry, and it made me even more excited to propose some of the new ideas John and I had come up with to my parents when they came home in February.

Eva was having a ball introducing Miles to all her women friends and telling the story of how Nana's box of things had been recovered from her crawl space. Miles had agreed to come for a visit just to attend the wine tasting party. I stood for a moment and looked around the room at all these people who had become so dear to me over the last six months. When you live under one roof and work side-by-side seven days a week, people become like family to you. I stood back and watched as folks smiled, laughed, and toasted each other. It was a heartwarming sight.

"Penny for your thoughts," John said, whispering the words in my ear, giving me goosebumps. Being near him in this newfound way was so endearing and made me feel loved. We had become closer than I imagined we would over the course of the month, sharing our innermost thoughts and secrets. We decided to share Thanksgiving with John's family since my own family wouldn't be able to make it.

"You know how to throw a good party," John's grandmother said, as she sat down in the chair next to me. "Thank you for inviting me."

"Of course," I said, bending down to kiss her cheek. "It wouldn't be a party without you and your family here."

Just then, John rang the little bell we purchased at an antique market and asked for everyone's attention. I couldn't imagine what he was going to say since we never talked about making any announcements at the wine tasting. I looked at him curiously, and he smiled at me in that John-is-up-to-something sort of way, and I folded my arms waiting to hear his speech.

"I wanted to thank you all for coming tonight. As many of you know, Milly has been planning this for over a month, and she

was thrilled to receive such a great response. Her mother, Lisa, started this tradition, and I think we need to thank both Lisa and Milly
for bringing us all together like this. In fact, I think we should thank
them both right here and right now with a toast..."

With that, my mother and father walked through the door,
and I found myself letting out a little screech of excitement. I ran
over to my mother and hugged her, my father enveloping us both
in an enormous embrace, while the guests cheered and clapped for
us all. When we let go after a minute, there was another surprise:
my sister, Cal, and Abbie were there, too—all of us reunited after
months and months apart.

"Thank you, John," my mother said finally, addressing the
group. "We certainly wouldn't be able to do what we do without you,
that's for sure. Thank you, everyone. Thanks for looking after the Inn,
thanks for looking after Milly, and we wish all of you a wonderful
Thanksgiving. Now, let's eat some of that fantastic food Colette has
lovingly prepared for us all. I can't wait to hug each one of you."

My mother pulled me aside first as the room burst into
sounds of chitter-chatter.

"So great to see you, honey. You look wonderful. Do we have
our old Milly back?" she asked.

"Yes," I said. "I'm sorry it took so long."

"Worth the wait. Plus, I got your father all to myself for six months, which wasn't so bad, either. It was like a second honey-moon—honestly," she said.

"No details, please," I said, smiling.

"I'm so glad for you and John. I'm so glad for you."

"Thank you," I said to her. "Your matchmaking may have paid off. And now you're back for good?"

"Yes," she said. "Back for good."

"Excellent because John and I have some big ideas for you. And my new house passed inspection. I can move in three weeks from now after I settle on it."

"All this happiness," my mother said. "I don't know if I can take it."

*

"So, I was thinking about what I read on your blog and the stories you've told me, and I think you should write the foreward to my book," Miles said.

"Me?"

"Yes, you, Hemingway. And after you write that, I think you should write the story about you and your grandmother—really tell the story now that you have a sturdy one to tell."

"I just may agree with you on that, Miles," I said.

"I do know a few people in the publishing world, you know. You may even get a book deal from the amazing details of your family, the Inn, and the parallel stories of you and your grandmother. You could even write it as fiction if you wanted to go crazy and get creative."

"Maybe, Miles, but I may have other hopes and dreams now."

"Who says you can't do it all?" he asked.

I smiled at him. "You know, I just may give it all a shot."

"There's the spirit," he said.

John approached the conversation and joined Miles and me. "Miles—any interest in going kayaking in the morning? Looks like it's going to be a nice day," John said.

Miles looked quite pleased by the invitation.

"Would love to do that," he said, "and in the spring, can you get me on a jet ski?"

*

Later that night, after the wine tasting was over and my mom and dad were tucked into the Queen Room until I moved into my new home, John and I were alone in his cottage.

"Close your eyes," he said.

I closed them.

"Put your hands out, palms facing each other, like you might grip a steering wheel," he said.

I held out my hands. He placed something in them, and arranged my hands so that I was holding the sides of it.

"Okay, the curiosity is killing me," I said. "Can I open them now?"

"Yes," he said.

I looked at the artwork. It was a painting of me on John's boat holding a camera and photographing the Inn from the water. I could tell it was from that day he patiently glided me around when I first came to the Inn and I needed pictures to update the website, the Nikon in my hand. I felt a lump build in my throat.

"You painted this? How?" I asked.

"You didn't know it, but I took a photo of you with my phone that day...and I just tried my best to replicate it."

"This is beautiful, John. I mean, it's really beautiful. I don't know what to say. Thank you."

I sat down on the chair next to John's desk and admired it some more. The lighting, the way my hair was blowing in the breeze, the sunlight at my back illuminating Inn Significant. I was in awe.

"I wanted to give it to you sooner, but I didn't want to make you feel uncomfortable about it. You were in your glory that afternoon, taking those shots, brainstorming the website idea. You look—"

"Happy," I said.

"Yes, because you were."

"Because I am," I said.

Epilogue

Afterword | Inn Significant
By Emelia (Milly) Foster

It's ironic sometimes what history teaches you when you have an open mind. Three and a half years ago, I wouldn't have been able to identify with someone else's story to help me get through my own marked misery, let alone write a book about it. However, that all changed when my now fiancé, John, found a journal that belonged to my grandmother in the basement of the Inn my family owns and operates. The similarities between my current life and the life of my late grandmother were freakishly alike; we suffered heartbreaking losses of our first husbands and were later matched with our subsequent loves by family and friends. To say history repeats itself, without a doubt, is somewhat true.

After my parents grew weary of seeing me in my pajamas with unwashed hair feeling sorry for myself years after my husband Gil's death, as a last-ditch effort, they asked me to come and run their Inn on the Eastern Shore of Maryland in a town named Oxford. I'd grown up visiting Oxford, as the house previously belonged to my grandparents. After their deaths, my parents decided the property would make a gorgeous and relaxing inn. They were so right.

When I somehow found the courage to write and tell my story, I tried my best to capture every detail. I hadn't written in years, so I had to rekindle my love for writing (with big pushes from loved ones) in order to do it and move on from tragedy. With encouragement from my friend Miles and his own publisher, I decided to tackle writing again and share my story with you. I am deeply indebted to Miles for several reasons: first, because he successfully dared me to come back from my depression and years of mourning to write again; second, because his stark candor allowed him to tell me how awful Inn Significant's website was, which forced an excellent collaboration between my sister and me to fix it; and third, because he had the sense to enlighten me to the wholly unfathomable notion at the time that love was waiting for me around the corner.

Along with Miles, I have to thank those closest to me for pulling me back to life: Colette, Darlene, Karen, Eva, and most importantly, my parents and John. I love you all very much. Thank you for your kindness, faith, patience, and unyielding support.

John and I still work with my parents at the Inn, and we live in that adorable house with the Victorian detail and flower boxes, which is just down the street from Inn Significant. The new venue that will house small wedding receptions is quickly approaching completion, and my mom and I will be coordinating those together. It's been incredibly therapeutic for me to continue my career as a writer, and John's been exhibiting and selling his paintings, in addition to teaching art classes nearby.

Our town may be small, but we are mighty. We rely on our neighbors and friends for support and to help us when times are tough, whether that means getting through the daily challenges of the Great Depression or overcoming the tragic loss of a husband. A place can, indeed, be wonderful, but it's the people who make it special.

My story is not unique; millions of people lose loved ones every day. In that sense, we are not alone. As for me, I'm grateful to my grandmother for putting her feelings down on paper. Her heartfelt storytelling about her life helped me understand my own grief, as I was able to relate directly to someone I always admired—someone who had experienced the same kind of loss and pain. Likewise, her approach to later finding happiness with my grandfather was just what I needed to hear, whether she ever intended for anyone to read her private thoughts or not.

Healing is never easy, but it is possible when you find yourself in a place with people who truly give a place its name: the significant people who make up my home at the Inn.

Book Club Questions

1. Some people can overcome the death of a loved one better than others, though no one would ever say it's an easy endeavor. Why do you think Milly struggled for so long to recover from Gil's passing?

2. We learn that Milly ended up leaving her job as a writer at a magazine after Gil's death because she couldn't find it within her to write again. How does that decision play into the rest of the story?

3. What does Milly learn about her mother and father during her time at the Inn that she may not have known when the story begins?

4. Rosa's journal is integral to Milly's recovery even though she learns things about her family history she did not know prior to working at the Inn. Does Milly resent the previously unknown information gleaned from Rosa's journal? Why do you think Rosa never told anyone about Ferio?

5. Milly makes a lot of connections with people in the story. Which of these connections do you believe is most vital to her recovery?

6. John and Milly both feel somewhat damaged by what has happend in each of their pasts. Do you think this is what brings them together?

7. Healing can be a step-by-step process. How do the various characters in Milly's life help her move on?

8. Have you ever had a friend like Miles who looks at things in a very pragmatic way and essentially tells you to "get on with life?" Explain.

9. The idea of feeling guilty for having lived while someone you loved dearly died is tough to grapple with on a daily basis. Do you think this is the crux of Milly's sadness?

10. How integral to the story is the setting of Inn Significant? Is there truth to the statement that a place can heal you? Why or why not.

Author's Notes

Once again, thank you so much for investing your time in this novel. There are many books from which to choose, and the fact that you chose mine to read means a great deal to me. *Grazie.*

As I typically do at the end of my novels, I like to offer a little insight as to why I wrote this piece of fiction, because I know as a reader myself, I like to learn as much as I can from writers about what motivates and feeds their stories. Unlike my other two previous novels, the first having been a short story that was in my head for over twenty years and finally blossomed into a novel, and the second having borrowed from my real life experiences working in professional baseball, this story was inspired by the idea of a place.

The truth is, I don't know anyone who owns an inn, and I've never lived on the Eastern Shore of Maryland. But the whole notion of it is entirely appealing to me—the idea of living on the water, waking up each day to a peaceful setting, being part of a small town community, making people happy, and of course, love in its many forms, found their way into the heart of this story. If you visit Oxford, Maryland, take a peek at the Sandaway Inn that is, in fact, perched on the Tred Avon River. Its setting was the inspiration for this story, as were many other aspects and places within the town. My mother and I spent a day in Oxford together doing a little research for this novel, and, as always, we both came away feeling enchanted.

I am also in awe of people who seem to recover from life-altering tragedies and come out of them triumphant, even if sadness comes with the package.

One of my writing idols, J.K. Rowling, said, "I just write what I want to write. I write what amuses me. It's totally for myself." I remember reading her quote years ago and thinking, yes! That's it! That's exactly it! I suppose what happens as writers is that we get lucky when someone else enjoys our work just as much as we enjoy creating it. (And in her case, she is the luckiest and most successful author on the planet.)

There are few things I love more than delving into that imaginative place where I can be someone else, think like someone else, and create someone else who is not me at all. That is the case with these characters. None of these characters is based on anyone I know in particular, but rather on a collection of life experiences and individuals I have encountered throughout my years.

Isn't it wonderful what our imaginations and reading can do for us? They take us away from our daily routines and offer us insight into places where we may never live, meet people we may never meet, and love people we may never love. As I said to one of my friends earlier today, "Life is better in fiction."

While it's certainly not always the case, sometimes I think it may very well be true.

~ Stephanie Verni

50370798R00168

Made in the USA
Middletown, DE
30 October 2017